U0132399

FAMOUS QUOTES
OF CHINESE WISDOM
漢英對照中國經典名句

劉士聰 谷啓楠 編譯

商務印書館

漢英對照中國經典名句
Famous Quotes of Chinese Wisdom

編　　譯：劉士聰　谷啟楠
責任編輯：黃家麗　王朴真
封面設計：張　毅
出　　版：商務印書館 (香港) 有限公司
　　　　　香港筲箕灣耀興道 3 號東滙廣場 8 樓
　　　　　http://www.commercialpress.com.hk
發　　行：香港聯合書刊物流有限公司
　　　　　香港新界大埔汀麗路 36 號中華商務印刷大廈 3 字樓
印　　刷：中華商務彩色印刷有限公司
　　　　　香港新界大埔汀麗路 36 號中華商務印刷大廈 14 字樓
版　　次：2016 年 10 月第 1 版第 2 次印刷
　　　　　©2014 商務印書館 (香港) 有限公司
　　　　　ISBN 978 962 07 0366 9
　　　　　Printed in Hong Kong
　　　　　版權所有　不得翻印

出版說明

　　本書從中國經典裏精選超過 500 條名句，分 15 個主題，其中包括：中國人的思考方式、傳統智慧、談人生、談處世，內容全面，另備筆畫索引供讀者快速查閱。

　　無論是孔子關於教與學的名句 "學而時習之，不亦說乎？" 或是司馬遷的忠告 "勇者不避難，智者不失時。"，書內均列明出處。

　　名句選自超過 120 個中國歷代著名人物，有詩人如李白把酒問月 "今人不見古時月，今月曾經照古人。"；有古代賢臣魏徵上諫君王 "善始者實繁，克終者蓋寡。"；也有李耳談永恆 "道可道，非常道；名可名，非常名。" 等。

　　另對疑難詞作出解釋，對精選條目提供評論，還對發音特殊的單字注漢語拼音。本書適合對中國智慧、中國文化有興趣的外國人、華裔人士，甚至本地讀者使用，也適合翻譯從業員用作參考書。

商務印書館編輯部

Publisher's Note

This title is a collection of over 500 Chinese quotes from Chinese classics, covering a wide range of 15 topics such as Chinese thinking, traditional wisdom, guidance regarding life, ways of the world, etc.

Whether you think over the words of, Confucius 'Isn't it a delightful thing to constantly apply what you've learned?,' or the advice of, Sima Qian 'Courageous people do not shun danger and crises, and wise people do not miss opportunities.', this title provides the answer to the questions 'Who said that?' and 'What can I learn?'

There are quotes from over 120 famous people, including classic quotes from established names such as Tang poet Li Bai, 'Today's people have not seen the ancient moon, but today's moon has shone on the ancient people.', ranging from the maxim of Wei Zheng for the ruler, 'Many people can begin well, but not many of them can end well.', to Li Er's view on eternality 'The Tao that can be described is not the eternal Tao; the Name that can be named is not the eternal name'.

Now featuring notes on difficult terms, comments on selected entries and supplementary Hanyu pinyin to clarify confusing pronunciations, this title is suitable for westerners, expatriates or even Chinese people who are interested in Chinese wisdom and Chinese culture. It is also an invaluable addition to translators' working libraries.

Editorial Department
The Commercial Press (H.K.) Ltd.

前　言

　　本書收錄名言警句，多選自中國古代哲學和文學著作，以及哲人和文人關於政治、人生、治學等方面的言論。這裏選取的只是中國古代浩如煙海典籍中的點滴，但涉及的內容豐富，思想深邃。雖然這些文字都是在古代歷史背景下寫的，但對我們仍有智慧及道德啟示，特別是某些道德準則正在消失的今天，重溫古人尊崇的一些價值觀是有意義的。凡對中國古代思想和傳統智慧有興趣的人讀來會感到趣味盎然，在關於生活、處世、治學等方面都有所啟發，這是編譯本書的初衷。

　　本書條目按內容分為 15 部分，為方便讀者查找，又將各條目編成筆畫索引，附於正文後面。為便於理解，除將漢語條目譯成英語，還對發音特殊的單字注漢語拼音，對疑難詞作出解釋，並對部分條目提供精要的註釋和評論。

　　由於編譯者的水平所限，所譯英語難免有不妥或錯誤之處，希望讀者指出，將來有機會再糾正。

編譯者

Preface

This title is a collection of Chinese witticisms from ancient famous Chinese philosophical and literary works and remarks by philosophers, writers and poets on politics, life, learning and writing. The current collection is but a drop in the ocean of the ancient Chinese classics, but it is already rich in content and profound in ideas. Though these selections were written under particular circumstances in different times over history, they still communicate words of great wisdom and moral messages to us today, especially when some of the moral values advertised by the ancients have, more or less, been melting away, it is meaningful to refresh our memory by reviewing the value system that our ancestors had upheld. It will prove to be an interesting title to people interested in ancient Chinese thinking and traditional wisdom, and guidance regarding life, the ways of the world and learning. This is what has prompted us to put this book together.

The entries in the book are classified into 15 parts according to their contents and meanings and a stroke index is provided at the end of the text for the convenience of the reader. In order to help the students understand better, besides translating the entries into English, we have also added Hanyu pinyin to the characters with pronunciations unfamiliar to today's readers, and made explanations to some difficult terms. For the same purpose, we have put in some brief notes to and comments on some of the entries.

As this is our first experience in compiling a book of this kind, there might be errors and mistranslations in it. We sincerely hope our readers will kindly point them out when any are found so that we can correct them when the book has a chance to be reprinted.

The Editors and Translators

目錄 Contents

出版說明 Publisher's Note i

前言 Preface iii

一 品德修養 Cultivate Moral Integrity

（一）樹德修身 Develop Morality and Mold Character 1

（二）持義守正 Uphold Justice and Maintain Honesty 8

（三）謙恭 Modesty 15

（四）誠信求實 Be Trustworthy and Realistic 19

（五）知止節慾 Exercise Restraint 22

（六）嚴己寬人 Be Strict with Yourself and Lenient
with Others 25

（七）大公無私 Be Unselfish 28

（八）知恥從善 Knowing What Is Shame and Following
What Is Good 30

（九）勇敢頑強 Be Courageous and Steadfast 34

二 處世 Get along with People

（一）謹慎 Be Prudent 37

（二）名利富貴 Be Indifferent to Fame and Fortune 45

（三）自強自立 Be Self-supporting 50

（四）獨善其身 Be Self-edifying 52

（五）隨遇而安 Adapt Oneself to Circumstances 54

（六）淡泊 Be Nonchalant to Worldly Concerns 56

（七）韜光養晦 Keep a Low Profile 58

（八）隱居歸田 Pastoral Life 62

（九）待人 Treating People the Right Way 63

三　識人 Understand People in Perspective

（一）知賢 Distinguish People by Virtue and Talent 66

（二）育人舉賢 Educate the People and Recommend
　　　the Virtuous 83

（三）量才授任 Designate Assignment According to
　　　Competence 91

（四）用眾成事 Make Concerted Efforts 94

（五）不求全責備 No One is Perfect 98

（六）不以尊卑長幼論人 One Should Not Be Judged by
　　　Age and Status 103

（七）不以貌取人 Looks Can Be Deceptive 106

（八）人老智可用 The Aged Has More Wisdom 108

（九）用人信人 Trust the Person Employed 109

（十）才能品德特別出眾者 Outstanding People 110

（十一）成才須磨練 Talent is Cultivated through Hardships 111

四　處境 Situations Make the Difference 114

五　世態人情 Ways of the World

（一）貧富懸殊 The Poor and the Rich 117

（二）世事滄桑 Vicissitudes of Life 121

六　納言 Accept to Good Advice

（一）博聽 Remain Open to Advice 124

（二）不因人取言 Make Judicious Judgments of
　　　One's Words 126

（三）以實核言 Respect Reality 127

（四）聽直排諛 Take Honest Words and Reject
　　　Flattering Ones.. 130

七　人倫關係 Human Relations 133

八　思想感情 Ideas and Feelings
　（一）愛國情懷 Patriotism 140
　（二）壯志凌雲 Soaring Ambitions 143
　（三）思人 Missing the Dear Ones 146
　（四）思鄉 Homesickness 148
　（五）別情 Part with Emotions and Return with
　　　Mixed Feelings... 151

九　思想方法 Way of Thinking
　（一）審時度勢 Take Stock of Situations 153
　（二）自知之明 View Oneself in Perspective 155

十　教育與學習 Education and Study
　（一）學習態度 Attitude toward Study 156
　（二）教與學 Teach and Learn 161
　（三）從師 Learn from the Teacher 164
　（四）教師 Teacher 166

十一　惜時 Cherish Time 168

十二　養生 Preserve Health 172

十三　哲理 Philosophical Concepts
　（一）轉化 Transformation 174
　（二）凡事有規律 Everything Has Its Own Course
　　　of Evolution 176
　（三）相對與絕對 Relative vs. Absolute 179

（四）實踐出真知 True Knowledge Comes from Practice 184

（五）權衡 Weigh and Measure 184

（六）道不可言，真理不滅 Tao and Truth 188

（七）善始善終 Begin Well and End Well 194

（八）果斷成事，猶豫無功 Be Decisive 195

（九）功以謀就 Think before You Act 197

（十）舉綱張目 Take the Key 198

（十一）由表及裏，由此及彼 From the Exterior to the Interior,

　　　　from One to the Other 199

十四　治國 Govern the Country

（一）民 The People 202

（二）居安思危，謹慎為政 Think of Peril in Peace and

　　　Exercise Prudence in Politics... 206

（三）為政有術 Art of Government 207

（四）鑒古知今 Learn from History 209

（五）忠於職守 Do Your Best to Carry out Your Duties 210

十五　文學藝術 Literature and Art

（一）文與行 Writing and Conduct 213

（二）風格 Style 216

筆畫索引 Stroke Index 219

一、 品德修養
Cultivate Moral Integrity

（一）樹德修身
Develop Morality and Mold Character

1. 達人無不可，忘己愛蒼生。　　——唐·王維《贈房盧氏琯》

A philosophical person can adapt himself to any circumstance; he forgets himself and gives his love to the common people.

—Wang Wei (701-761; 698-759), poet of the Tang Dynasty

Terms:
a. 達人：通達事理的人 a philosophical person
b. 無不可：隨遇而安；能適應各種情況 to be able to adapt oneself to circumstances
c. 忘己：忘掉自己 to forget oneself; to be selfless
d. 蒼生：百姓 the common people

2. 見其生，不忍見其死；聞其聲，不忍食其肉。
是以君子遠庖廚也。　　——《孟子·梁惠王上》

When you've seen how birds and animals live, you cannot bear to see them killed; when you've heard how birds chirp and animals cry, you cannot bear to eat their meat. Therefore, a man of honour has his kitchen placed out of sight and hearing (or keeps away from his kitchen).

—Mencius by Meng Ke (c.372-289 BC), philosopher and Confucian scholar of the Warring States Period

Terms:

a. 生：活着 to live; be alive
b. 不忍：不忍心 cannot bear to
c. 是以：所以 therefore
d. 遠：使遠離 to place something at a distance
e. 庖（páo）廚：廚房 kitchen
f. 君子：The term "君子" was used more frequently in ancient times. As it has no equivalent in English, it has been translated into English in different ways, such as "a man of noble character", "a noble man", "a man of moral integrity", "people of moral character", "virtuous people", "honourable people", "a man of moral integrity", "an honourable person", "a man of honour", and "an honourable man". It is also transliterated as *junzi*, for the sake of accuracy. Although the English word "gentleman" has a similar connotation, it is not identical.

Comment: As Mencius believes that man is good by nature, he extends his compassion for man to birds and animals.

3. 不失其所者久，死而不亡者壽。

——《老子·道經三十三》

He who does not abandon his fundamental principles will last long, and he whose Tao does not fade away after death enjoys a real long life.

—Laozi by Li Er（李耳）*, philosopher of late Spring and Autumn Period, and founder of Taoism*

Terms:

a. 久（jiǔ）：長久 to last long
b. 亡：指"道"的消亡 the fading away of Tao
c. 壽：長壽 long life

Comment: It emphasizes that only sages do not abandon their Tao. It also suggests that people with lofty spirit and people who have created great theories survive their death.

4. 德如寒泉，假有沙塵，弗能污也。

——北齊‧劉晝《劉子‧通塞》

Moral virtue is like clear spring water. It cannot be soiled by sand or dust.

—Liuzi by Liu Zhou (514 – 565), writer of the Northern Qi Dynasty

Terms:

a. 德：道德　(moral) virtue
b. 寒泉：清澈的泉水 clear spring water
c. 假：假如 even if
d. 弗能：不能 cannot

5. 以德防患，憂禍不存。

——漢‧焦贛《焦氏易林》

1) When you take moral cultivation as a precaution against trouble, misfortune will not occur.
2) When you prevent trouble from happening with moral influence, misfortune can be prevented.

—Jiao Gong of the Han Dynasty

Terms:

a. 患（huàn）：災禍 trouble; disaster
b. 憂禍：憂患 trouble; misfortune
c. 生：發生 to occur; to happen; to emerge

Comment: To prevent trouble from occurring, some people prefer to resort to money, power, or even weapons, but it is believed that moral influence is more effective.

6. 君子以多識前言往行，以畜其德。

——《周易‧大畜》

A man of honour should remember the good things ancient people said and did, so as to cultivate his own moral integrity accordingly.

—The Book of Changes, a Confucian classic

Terms:

a. 識（zhì）：通 "志"，記住 to remember
b. 前言往行：前人的言行 remarks and deeds by ancient people
c. 畜：培養 to cultivate / nurture / foster (virtue)
d. 君子：a man of honour = an honourable man

7. 君子疾沒世而名不稱焉。   ——《論語・衛靈公》

What worries an honourable man is that he has failed to leave a good name behind after death.

> —*The Analects, a Confucian classic recording the words and deeds of Confucius and his dialogues with his disciples*

Terms:

a. 疾：恐怕 to worry
b. 沒（mò）：通 "歿"（mò）death
c. 沒世：死後 after death
d. 稱：稱頌 to praise

8. 君子所求者，沒世之名；今人所求者，當世之名。

——清・顧炎武《答李紫瀾書》

Ancient *junzi* cared about posthumous fame, whereas people today seek rise in fame while alive.

> —*Gu Yanwu (1613-1682), scholar and thinker of late Ming and early Qing Dynasty*

Terms:

a. 君子 *junzi* = an honourable man

Comment: Those who seek instant fame actually seek prompt interests.

9. 大人者，不失其赤子之心者也。　　——《孟子‧離婁下》

A man of lofty moral integrity is one who maintains the pure heart of a newborn baby.

> —Mencius by Meng Ke (c.372 – 289 BC), philosopher
> and Confucian scholar of the Warring States Period

Terms:

a. 大人：品德高尚的人 men of high moral standard

b. 赤子：初生嬰兒 newborn babies; virgin and innocent infants

Comment: This is high praise for people of lofty moral integrity.

10. 德不孤，必有鄰。　　——《論語‧里仁》

A virtuous person is not lonely. He will have friendly companions with him.

> —The Analects, a Confucian classic recording the words and
> deeds of Confucius and his dialogues with his disciples

Terms:

a. 孤：孤單 lonely; solitary

b. 鄰：親近的人 companions

11. 道高益安，勢高益危。　　——《史記‧日者列傳》

Moral virtue makes one safer, and high status leaves one exposed to vulnerabilities.

> —Historical Records by Sima Qian (c.145 or 135 – ? BC) of
> the Han Dynasty

Terms:

a. 道：品德 moral virtue

b. 勢：地位 status

c. 益：更；越發 the more

Comment: One should always remember to cultivate his moral integrity instead of seeking high status.

12. 上善若水。 ——《老子‧道經八》

The temperament of a superior person is like water.

—Laozi by Li Er（李耳）, *philosopher of late Spring and Autumn Period, and founder of Taoism*

Terms: 上善：具有完善品格的人 a superior person

Comment: Laozi believes that water benefits ten thousand other things but does not contend with them. It chooses to flow toward low places, but it never complains. It can fit in containers of any form, round or cubic. It adapts itself to circumstances, and it is essential to life. Water has the highly-esteemed quality.

13. 善人富，謂之賞；淫人富，謂之殃。 ——《左傳‧襄公二十八年》

When a good man becomes wealthy, it is a reward bestowed by Heaven; when a vicious man becomes wealthy, it is a disaster imposed upon him by Heaven.

—Zuo Zhuan, first chronological history covering the period from 722 BC to 464 BC, attributed to Zuo Qiuming

Terms:
a. 善人：好人 a good person
b. 富：富有 rich; wealthy
c. 賞：賞賜 a reward
d. 淫人：邪惡的人 a vicious man
e. 殃：災禍 disasters

Comment: When a vicious person becomes rich by dishonest means, bad luck is likely to come upon him.

14. 桃李不言，下自成蹊。　　　——《史記‧李將軍列傳》

Although peach and plum trees never attract people
with speech, there are trodden paths under them.

*—Historical Records by Sima Qian (c.145 or 135 – ? BC) of
the Han Dynasty*

Terms:
a. 桃：桃樹 peach tree
b. 李：李樹 plum tree
c. 蹊 (xī)：小路 path; trail

Comment: People who do not praise themselves have an
attractive force.

15. 知者不惑，仁者不憂，勇者不懼。　——《論語‧子罕》

Wise people have no bafflement, humane people have
no worries, and brave people have no fears.

*—The Analects, a Confucian classic recording
the words and deeds of Confucius and his dialogues with his disciples*

Terms:
a. 知者："知" 通 "智"，有智慧的人 wise people
b. 仁者：有仁德的人 humane people
c. 勇者：勇敢的人 brave / courageous people

16. 有德不可敵。　　　——《左傳‧僖公二十八年》

A virtuous person cannot be opposed.

*—Zuo Zhuan, first chronological history covering the
period from 722 BC to 464 BC, attributed to Zuo Qiuming*

Terms:
a. 有德：有德的人 virtuous people
b. 不可敵：不可對抗 cannot be opposed

17. 志士仁人，無求生以害仁，有殺身以成仁。

——《論語‧衛靈公》

People with moral integrity and noble aspirations do not sacrifice humaneness for life, but sacrifice life for humaneness.

— The Analects, a Confucian classic recording the words and deeds of Confucius and his dialogues with his disciples

Terms:
a. 志士仁人：具有高尚品德和遠大志向的人 people with moral integrity and noble aspirations
b. 求生以害仁：為了保全自己的生命而損害仁德 to sacrifice humaneness for life
c. 殺身以成仁：為了仁德而犧牲生命 to sacrifice life for humaneness

（二）持義守正
Uphold Justice and Maintain Honesty

1. 人固有一死，或重於泰山，或輕於鴻毛。

——漢‧司馬遷《報任安書》

All men will die, but death could be weightier than Mount Tai, or lighter than a feather.

— "A Letter to Ren An" by Sima Qian (c.145 or 135 – ? BC) of the Han Dynasty

Terms:
a. 泰山：山名，在今山東省，常比喻受人尊重的人或重大的事 Mount Tai, a mountain in Shandong Province, often referred to as a metaphor for respectable people or significant things
b. 鴻毛：鴻雁的羽毛，比喻輕，或不重要 goose feather, used as a metaphor for insignificant things

Comment: This is from a letter Sima Qian wrote to his friend Ren An. It has been frequently quoted and re-quoted ever since.

Mao Zedong, quoting it in his article "Serve the People" (Sept. 8, 1944), says, "To die for the people is weightier than Mount Tai, but to work for the fascists and die for the exploiters or oppressors is lighter than a feather. Comrade Chang Szuteh died for the people, and his death is indeed weightier than Mount Tai." (*Selected Works of Mao Tse-tung*, vol. III, p.177)

2. 生而辱，不如死而榮。　　　——《史記·范雎蔡澤列傳》

Die a glorious death rather than live a disgraceful life.

—Historical Records by Sima Qian (c.145 or 135 – ? BC) of
the Han Dynasty

3. 見義不為，無勇也。　　　——《論語·為政》

1) If one remains indifferent to the call of a just cause, he is a coward.
2) If one takes no action at the call of a just cause, he is a coward.

—The Analects, a Confucian classic recording the words and
deeds of Confucius and his dialogues with his disciples

Terms:
a. 義：合乎正義的事情 righteousness; a just cause
b. 為：做 to act; to take action; to do

Comment: This indicates what Confucius expects a man of honour to do.

4. 生亦我所欲也，義亦我所欲也；二者不可得兼，
舍生而取義者也。　　　——《孟子·告子上》

Life is what I want, and so is righteousness. If it is impossible to have both, I would give up my life for righteousness.

—Mencius by Meng Ke (c.372 – 289 BC), philosopher
and Confucian scholar of the Warring States Period

Terms:

a. 欲：要 to want
b. 得兼：得到兩者（即 "生" 和 "義"）to have both
c. 舍：捨棄 to give up; to abandon; to relinquish

5. 君子死義，不可以富貴留也。　　　——《文子・九守》

A man of honour would rather die for righteousness than live for wealth and rank.

—Wenzi, a Taoist work by unknown author of
the Warring States Period

Terms:

a. 死義：為義而死 to die for righteousness
b. 富貴：富有而尊貴 riches and honour; wealth and rank
c. 留：活着 to live; to stay alive
d. 君子：a man of honour = an honourable man

Comment: To die for righteousness or to live for wealth and rank, this distinguishes an honourable person from a mean and selfish one.

6. 君子陷人於危，必同其難。　　　——《漢晉春秋》

When a man of honour has someone ended up in trouble, he will go through the trouble with him.

—A Chronicle from Eastern Han Dynasty to Western Jin Dynasty by
Xi Zaochi (? – 383), historian of the Eastern Jin Dynasty

Terms:

a. 危：危難 trouble, a difficult or dangerous situation
b. 君子：a man of honour = an honourable man

7. 以義死難，視死如歸。　　　——《史記‧范雎蔡澤列傳》

It is like home coming to die for righteousness under adverse or dangerous circumstances.

—Historical Records by Sima Qian (c.145 or 135 – ? BC) of the Han Dynasty

Terms:
a. 死難：死於危難 to die in adversity
b. 如歸：如同回家 like home-coming

8. 有事不避難，有罪不避刑。　　　——《國語‧晉語七》

Don't try to escape the consequences of a contingency you are involved in, and don't try to evade the punishment for the crime you have committed.

—Remarks of Monarchs, history of late Western Zhou Dynasty and other major states in the Spring and Autumn Period, attributed to Zuo Qiuming, historian of the State of Lu

9. 石可破也，而不可奪堅；丹可磨也，而不可奪赤。

——《呂氏春秋‧誠廉》

1) Stone can be smashed, but never loses its hard quality; cinnabar can be ground, but never loses its red colour.
2) You can smash the stone, but you cannot change its hardness; you can grind the cinnabar, but you cannot change its redness.

—Lü's Spring and Autumn Annuals, compiled under the sponsorship of Lü Buwei, Prime Minister of the State of Qin during the late Warring States Period

Comment: This is a metaphor, meaning that the moral principles of an honourable man cannot be changed.

10. 石赤不奪，節士之必。　　　　　——漢・揚雄《太玄・度》

1) A man of integrity must have the qualities of stone and cinnabar that never change their nature.

2) He who is by nature like stone that does not change its hardness and cinnabar that does not change its redness must be a man of moral integrity.

—Yang Xiong (53 BC – 18 AD), writer and philosopher of the Western Han Dynasty

Terms:

a. 石赤：石頭和朱砂 stone and cinnabar

b. 節士：有節操的人 a man of integrity

11. 君子不宛言而取富，不屈行而取位。

——《大戴禮記・曾子制言中》

A noble man does not try to attain wealth with blandishments, nor does he try to acquire official positions by dishonest means.

—Da Dai's Book of Rites compiled by Dai De, scholar on rites of the Western Han Dynasty

Terms:

a. 宛言：花言巧語 blandishments

b. 屈行：不正直的行為 by dishonest means; in dishonest ways

c. 取位：取得官職 to acquire official positions

d. 君子：a noble man = an honourable man

12. 富與貴，是人之所欲也，不以其道得之，不處也；貧與賤，是人之所惡也，不以其道得之，不去也。

——《論語・里仁》

Wealth and high social status are desired, but they should not be accepted unless they are obtained by appropriate means; poverty and low social status are detested, but they should not be evaded unless they are shaken off by appropriate means.

—The Analects, a Confucian classic recording
the words and deeds of Confucius and his dialogues with his disciples

Terms:

a. 欲：慾望 to desire; to long for
b. 道：正當的方法 (in this context) appropriate ways
c. 處（chǔ）：接受 to accept
d. 惡（wù）：厭惡 to detest; to abhor
e. 得：第一個"得"，得到的意思 to attain
　　第二個"得"，實為"去"，擺脫掉 to get rid of; to shake off

13. 言不取苟合，行不取苟容。　——《史記·范雎蔡澤列傳》

Do not say anything just to be in accord with others; do not do anything just to ingratiate yourself with others.

—Historical Records by Sima Qian (c.145
or 135 – ? BC) of the Han Dynasty

Terms:

a. 苟合：苟且附和 to be in accord with others
b. 苟容：苟且取悅 to ingratiate oneself with others

14. 君子上交不諂，下交不瀆。　——《周易·繫辭下》

An honourable man does not curry favour with his superior, nor does he look down upon his inferior.

—The Book of Changes, a Confucian classic

Terms:

a. 諂（chǎn）：奉承；討好 to curry favour with
b. 瀆（dú）：輕慢不敬 to look down upon

15. 無為其所不為，無欲其所不欲。　　——《孟子·盡心上》

Don't do anything you are not supposed to do, and don't take anything you are not supposed to take.

—Mencius by Meng Ke (c.372 – 289 BC), philosopher
and Confucian scholar of the Warring States Period

16. 南金不為處幽而自輕，瑾瑤不以居深而止潔。

——《抱朴子·廣譬》

1) Hidden in obscure places, genuine gold does not lose its weight; buried underground, beautiful jade does not lose its luster.
2) Genuine gold does not lose its weight because it is hidden in obscure places; beautiful jade does not lose its luster because it is buried underground.

—Baopuzi by Ge Hong (284 – 364) of the East Jin Dynasty

Terms:
a. 南金：南方出產的金子，真金 genuine gold
b. 瑾瑤：美玉 beautiful jade

17. 君子貞而不諒。　　——《論語·衛靈公》

An honourable man is honest and determined, but not stubborn.

—The Analects, a Confucian classic recording
the words and deeds of Confucius and his dialogues with his disciples

Terms:
a. 貞：正直堅定 honest and determined
b. 諒：固執 stubborn

18. 惻隱之心，人皆有之；羞惡之心，人皆有之；
　　恭敬之心，人皆有之；是非之心，人皆有之。

—《孟子・告子上》

Everyone has a sense of compassion; everyone has a
sense of shame; everyone has a sense of respect;
and everyone has a sense of right and wrong.

*—Mencius by Meng Ke (c.372 – 289 BC), philosopher
and Confucian scholar of the Warring States Period*

Terms:
a. 惻隱：同情 compassion; to show compassion
b. 羞惡：羞恥 shame

（三） 謙恭
Modesty

1. 滿招損，謙受益。　　　　　　—《尚書・大禹謨》

1) Complacency does you harm and modesty does you
good.
2) Complacency makes you fail, while modesty leads
you to success.
3) Be complacent and you have something to lose; be
modest and you have everything to gain.

—Collection of Ancient Texts, a Confucian classic

Terms:
a. 滿：自滿 complacency
b. 損：損害 harm
c. 謙：謙虛 modesty
d. 益：好處 benefit; to do someone good

2.   願無伐善，無施勞。   ——《論語・公冶長》

I would not brag about my merits, nor would I boast of
the good services I have rendered.

*—The Analects, a Confucian classic recording
the words and deeds of Confucius and his dialogues with his disciples*

Terms:

a. 伐善：誇耀自己的優點 to brag about one's merits

b. 施勞：誇耀自己的功勞 to boast of the good services one has done

3.   人之患，在好為人師。   ——《孟子・離婁上》

Some people have the weakness that they like to
lecture others.

*—Mencius by Meng Ke (c.372 – 289 BC), philosopher
and Confucian scholar of the Warring States Period*

Terms:

a. 患：缺點；毛病 weakness; defects

b. 好（hào）：喜歡〔貶義〕to like [derogatory]

4.   下士者得賢，下敵者得友，下眾者得譽。

                    ——《尸子・明堂》

He who adopts a humble attitude toward *shi* wins over
virtuous and capable people; he who adopts a humble
attitude toward his foes turns them into friends; he
who adopts a humble attitude toward the masses wins
their praises.

*—Shizi by Shi Jiao (c.390 – 330), thinker
and statesman of the Warring States Period*

Terms:

a. 下：對人謙恭 to be humble and modest to others

b. 士：在古代中國指大夫和庶民之間階層的人，也指知識分子和
學者 In ancient China, shi referred to the social stratum between

senior officials and the common people; it also referred to intellectuals as a whole and scholars. It is transliterated here.

c. 賢：賢才 virtuous and capable people

d. 譽：稱讚 to praise

5. 自伐者無功，功成者墮，名成者虧。 ──《莊子‧山木》

He who boasts of himself cannot succeed. Even if he does succeed, his success is sure to turn to failure, and even if he rises to fame, his fame is sure to wane.

—Zhuangzi by Zhuang Zhou (c.369 – 286 BC)
and his followers of the Warring States Period

Terms:

a. 自伐：自誇 to boast of oneself

b. 功：成功 to succeed

c. 墮 (huī)：失敗 to fail

d. 虧：敗落 to wane

6. 有餘則不泰，不足則自如。

──宋‧黃晞《聱隅子‧大中篇》

When you have enough and to spare, do not indulge with it; when you find yourself under scanty circumstances, try to adapt yourself to it and feel at ease with it.

—Huang Xi of the Northern Song Dynasty

Terms:

a. 不泰：不驕傲；不放縱 not to be complacent; not to indulge oneself

b. 自如：自適 to feel at ease

7. 勞而不伐，有功而不德，厚之至也。

——《周易·繫辭上》

1) Although one has rendered great services, he does not boast of himself; although he has performed great deeds, he does not expect others to be grateful to him. This is true loyalty and sincerity.

2) Having rendered great services, he does not praise himself; having performed great deeds, he does not expect to be thanked. This is where loyalty and sincerity culminate.

—<i>The Book of Changes, a Confucian classic</i>

Terms:

a. 勞：功勞 good services rendered
b. 伐：誇 to boast of
c. 德：感德，動詞，指 "要別人感謝" to expect others to show gratitude
d. 厚：忠厚 loyalty and sincerity

8. 富而不吝，寵而不驕。　—— 三國·魏·曹植《黃初六年令》

Rich but not stingy, favoured but not arrogant.

—<i>Cao Zhi (192 – 232), poet of the
State of Wei of the Three Kingdoms</i>

Terms:

a. 吝：吝嗇 to be stingy
b. 寵：受到寵愛 to be favoured

（四）誠信求實
Be Trustworthy and Realistic

1. 至信之人可以感物也。　　　　　　——《列子‧黃帝篇》

A man with noble sincerity can move inanimate things.

—Liezi, a Taoist classical work by Lie Yukou
of the Warring States Period

Terms:
a. 至信之人：最誠實的人 the most sincere people
b. 物：外物 inanimate things

2. 聲希者，響必巨；辭寡者，信必著。

——《抱朴子‧廣譬》

A quiet voice echoes loud; he who weighs his words has high prestige.

—Baopuzi by Ge Hong (284 – 364) of the East Jin Dynasty

Terms:
a. 希：稀疏 referring to voices or sounds that are quiet / slight
b. 響：迴聲 echo
c. 辭寡者：言語少的人 man of few words; man who weighs his words
d. 信必著：信用高 to have high prestige

3. 言必信，行必果。　　　　　　——《論語‧子路》

Keep your promise and be resolute in what you do.

—The Analects, a Confucian classic recording
the words and deeds of Confucius and his dialogues with his disciples

Terms:
a. 信：信用 to keep promise
b. 果：果敢 be resolute

4. 君子以言有物而行有恆。　　　——《周易‧家人‧象》

A man of honour should have substance in what he
says and be persistent in what he does.

—The Book of Changes, a Confucian classic

Terms:
a. 有物：言之有物；不說空話 to have content / substance in one's
talk
b. 有恆：持之以恆 be persistent
c. 君子：a man of honour = an honourable man

5. 人非信不立。　　　——北齊‧劉晝《劉子‧履信》

He who is lacking in good faith cannot establish
himself in society.

—Liuzi by Liu Zhou (514 – 565), writer of the Northern Qi Dynasty

Terms:
a. 非：沒有 without; to have not
b. 信：誠信 good faith
c. 立：立身 to establish oneself

6. 古者言之不出，恥躬之不逮也。　　　——《論語‧里仁》

Ancients were cautious about making commitments,
for they believed it was a disgrace if they failed to
fulfill them.

*—The Analects, a Confucian classic recording
the words and deeds of Confucius and his dialogues with his disciples*

Terms:
a. 古者：古代的人 ancients
b. 躬：自己 oneself
c. 不逮 (dài)：做不到 be unable to fulfill

7. 大人不華，君子務實。 ——漢・王符《潛夫論・敘錄》

Honourable people are not ostentatious; people of moral integrity are realistic.

*—Social Evils through the Eye of a Hermit by Wang Fu
(c.85 – 162), philosopher of the Eastern Han Dynasty*

Terms:

a. 大人：品德高尚的人 honourable people
b. 華：虛華，表面好看 ostentatious
c. 務：追求 to go for
d. 君子：people of moral integrity = honourable people

8. 白玉不雕，美珠不文，質有餘也。

——《淮南子・說林訓》

White jade does not need to be cut and polished, and genuine pearls do not need to be ornamented; they have far superior intrinsic qualities.

*—Huainanzi by Prince Huainan Liu An (179–122 BC)
and some of his followers of the Western Han Dynasty*

Terms:

a. 雕：雕琢 to cut and polish
b. 文（wén）：修飾 to ornament
c. 質：品質 quality

9. 君子恥其言而過其行。 ——《論語・憲問》

A man of honour believes it is a disgrace to say more and do less.

*—The Analects, a Confucian classic recording
the words and deeds of Confucius and his dialogues with his disciples*

Terms:

a. 恥：以……為恥 to take something as a disgrace
b. 君子：a man of honour = an honourable man

10. 當仁不讓於師。 ——《論語·衛靈公》

If it is in conformity with the humane spirit, you need not be too modest with your master.

*—The Analects, a Confucian classic recording
the words and deeds of Confucius and his dialogues with his disciples*

11. 知之為知之，不知為不知，是知也。 ——《論語·為政》

When you know, say you know; when you don't, say you don't. That is a sensible attitude.

*—The Analects, a Confucian classic recording
the words and deeds of Confucius and his dialogues with his disciples*

Terms:
a. "知之" 和 "不知" 中的 "知" 是 "知道、懂得" 之意 to know; to understand
b. "是知也" 中的 "知" 是 "聰明" 之意 sensible

12. 反身而誠，樂莫大焉。 ——《孟子·盡心上》

Nothing is more comforting than to find yourself an honest person on self-examination.

*—Mencius by Meng Ke (c.372 – 289 BC), philosopher
and Confucian scholar of the Warring States Period*

（五）知止節慾
Exercise Restraint

1. 知足者富，強行者有志。 ——《老子·道經三十三》

A contented man finds himself in abundance;
a hard-working man has a self-determined will.

*—Laozi by Li Er (李耳), philosopher of late Spring
and Autumn Period, and founder of Taoism*

Terms:
強行：努力做事的人 a hard-working man

2. 知足者，不以利自累也；審自得者，失之而不懼；
   行修於內者，無位而不怍。 ——《莊子‧讓王》

A contented man never encumbers himself with
wealth and position; he who knows how to make
himself happy is not afraid of losing what he desires;
a highly-cultured man does not feel ashamed when he
has no rank or title conferred on him.

*—Zhuangzi by Zhuang Zhou (c.369 – 286 BC)
and his followers of the Warring States Period*

Terms:
a. 自累：自己拖累自己 to encumber oneself
b. 審：懂得；明白 to know
c. 之：指想得到的東西 the thing one desires
d. 行修於內者：思想修養很好的人 a highly-cultured person
e. 怍 (zuò)：慚愧 be ashamed of

3. 知足不辱，知止不殆。 ——《老子‧德經四十四》

If one remains contented, he does not get humiliated;
if one knows when and where to hold off, he is not
exposed to vulnerabilities.

*—Laozi by Li Er (李耳), philosopher of late Spring
and Autumn Period, and founder of Taoism*

Terms:
a. 辱：受到侮辱 to be humiliated
b. 殆 (dài)：危險 in danger

4.   自信者不可以誹譽遷也，知足者不可以勢利誘也。

—— 《淮南子・詮言訓》

A self-confident man cannot be changed by slander or praise; a contented man cannot be tantalized with power or riches.

—Huainanzi by Prince Huainan Liu An (179 – 122 BC)
and some of his followers of the Western Han Dynasty

Terms:
a. 誹譽：誹謗和讚譽 slander and praise
b. 誘：誘惑 to tantalize

5.   情勝欲者昌，欲勝情者亡。   —— 《淮南子・繆稱訓》

When reason overcomes desires, one flourishes; when desires overcome reason, one perishes.

—Huainanzi by Prince Huainan Liu An (179 – 122 BC)
and some of his followers of the Western Han Dynasty

Terms:
a. 情：理智 reason
b. 欲：慾望 desire
c. 勝：戰勝 to overcome
d. 昌：昌盛 to flourish
e. 亡：滅亡 to perish

（六）嚴己寬人
Be Strict with Yourself and Lenient with Others

1. 古之至人，先存諸己而後存諸人。 ——《莊子・人間世》

In ancient times, highly-honourable people tried to cultivate their own moral integrity first, and then helped others to do so.

—Zhuangzi by Zhuang Zhou (c.369 – 286 BC)
and his followers of the Warring States Period

Terms:
a. 至人：修養極高之人 highly-honourable people
b. 存：樹立 to cultivate one's integrity

2. 君子不以其所能者病人，不以人之所不能者愧人。

——《禮記・表記》

A man of honour does not blame others for being incapable of what he can do, nor does he embarrass others for what they cannot do.

—The Book of Rites, a Confucian classic

Terms:
a. 病：責怪 to blame
b. 愧：使……難堪 to embarrass
c. 君子：a man of honour = an honourable man

3. 君子恥不修，不恥見污；恥不信，不恥不見信；
恥不能，不恥不見用。 ——《荀子・非十二子》

An honourable man takes it as a disgrace when he fails to cultivate his mind and character, but he does not think of it as such when he is humiliated; an honourable man takes it as a disgrace when he has no good faith, but he does not think of it as such when he is mistrusted; an honourable man takes it as a disgrace when he is incompetent, but he does not think of it as such when he is not appointed to office.

—Xunzi by Xun Kuang (313 – 238 BC), thinker and educator of the Warring States Period

Terms:
a. 恥：以……為恥 to take something as a disgrace
b. 修：修身，修養自己的品德 to cultivate one's integrity
c. 見：被 a form word used in passive voice
d. 信：第一個 "信" 是 "信義" good faith; credibility
　　　第二個 "信" 是 "信任" trust

4.　以得為在民，以失為在己；以正為在民，以枉為在己。

——《莊子・則陽》

The credit for success should be given to the people, and the responsibility for failure should be taken by yourself. If something is done in the right way, the credit should be given to the people; if something is done in the wrong way, the responsibility for the mistake should be taken by yourself.

—Zhuangzi by Zhuang Zhou (c.369 – 286 BC) and his followers of the Warring States Period

Terms:
a. 得：成功 success
b. 失：失敗 failure
c. 正：正確的做法 to do something the right way
d. 枉：錯誤的做法 to do something the wrong way

5. 古之君子，其責己也重以周，其待人也輕以約。

—— 唐 • 韓愈《原毀》

In ancient times, people of moral character set a high standard for themselves: they were strict with themselves and had all-round abilities, but they treated others in a generous and modest manner.

—Han Yu (768 – 824), writer and philosopher of the Tang Dynasty

Terms:

a. 責己：要求自己 to set a high standard for oneself
b. 重：嚴格 be strict
c. 周：全面 all-round
d. 輕：寬厚 be lenient; be generous
e. 約：簡約 simple; modest
f. 君子：people of moral character = honourable people

6. 善則稱人，過則稱己。   —— 《禮記 • 坊記》

1) Praise others for the good things they have done, and admit the mistakes you yourself have made.
2) Honour credit to others for the good things they have done, and admit the mistakes you yourself have made.

—The Book of Rites, a Confucian classic

Terms:

a. 善則稱人：稱讚別人的善行 to praise the good things others have done
b. 過則稱己：承認自己的過錯 to admit the mistakes you yourself have made

（七）大公無私
Be Unselfish

1. 君子不惜身以殉天下，但欲天下有利於我之殉耳。

——明·莊元臣

An honourable man is willing to sacrifice himself for
the country, and he only wishes that the people of the
country will benefit from his sacrifice.

—Zhuang Yuanchen (1560 – 1609) of the Ming Dynasty

Terms:

a. 殉：為……而犧牲 to sacrifice oneself for ...
b. 但：只；僅僅 only
c. 於：從 from

2. 非其罪，雖累辱而不愧也。   ——《史記·日者列傳》

An honourable man does not feel ashamed of himself
even if he is repeatedly wronged for mistakes he has
not committed.

—Historical Records by Sima Qian (c.145
or 135 – ? BC) of the Han Dynasty

Terms:

a. 罪：過錯 fault; mistake
b. 累：屢次 repeatedly

3. 君子有終身之樂，無一日之憂。   ——《荀子·子道》

An honourable man lives his whole life in happiness,
but he never worries himself for a single day.

—Xunzi by Xun Kuang (313 – 238 BC), thinker
and educator of the Warring States Period

4. 君子不憂不懼。 ── 《論語·顏淵》

An honourable man has nothing to worry about and
nothing to be afraid of.

*—The Analects, a Confucian classic recording
the words and deeds of Confucius and his dialogues with his disciples*

5. 平生不解藏人善，到處逢人說項斯。 ── 唐·楊敬之《贈項斯》

Never in my life have I neglected any talent,
So I tell stories about Xiang Si everywhere I go.

—Yang Jingzhi, poet of the Tang Dynasty

Terms:

a. 解：懂得 to know
b. 藏：埋沒 to neglect
c. 項斯：唐朝詩人 a poet of the Tang Dynasty

Note:

This is from a poem in praise of Xiang Si by Yang Jingzhi, the
official in charge of the Imperial College of the Tang Dynasty.
It was said that once a young poet came from the south to
Chang'an, the capital of the Tang Dynasty, seeking for an
interview with Yang Jingzhi. After Yang had read his poems and
met him in person, he was deeply impressed by his poems, and
even more impressed by his refined personality. Yang believed he
had the potential to become a talented poet, hence writing this
poem to praise and encourage him.

（八）知恥從善
Knowing What is Shame and Following What Is Good

1. 人不可以無恥，無恥之恥，無恥矣。

——《孟子·盡心上》

1) One should not be without a sense of shame. Ignorance of what is shameful is really shameful.

2) One should not be without a sense of shame. What is really shameful is ignorance of what is shameful.

—Mencius by Meng Ke (c.372 – 289 BC), philosopher and Confucian scholar of the Warring States Period

Terms:

a. 無恥：不知羞恥 with no sense of shame

b. 無恥之恥：不知羞恥之可恥 the fact that one doesn't know what is shameful is shameful

2. 吾日三省吾身。　　　　　——《論語·學而》

I examine myself on my moral integrity several times a day.

—The Analects, a Confucian classic recording the words and deeds of Confucius and his dialogues with his disciples

3. 朝過夕改，君子與之。　　——《漢書·宣元六王傳》

If mistakes made in the morning are rectified in the evening, it will be appreciated by honourable people.

—History of Han, chronicle of the Han Dynasty between 206 BC and 23 AD by Ban Gu (32 – 92)

Terms:

a. 朝（zhāo）：早晨 morning; in the morning

b. 與：讚許 to appreciate

4. 悟已往之不諫，知來者之可追。實迷途其未遠，
覺今是而昨非。　　　　　—— 晉・陶淵明《歸去來兮辭》

Now I know it's not possible to remedy the past, But
there's time to do better in the future. Fortunately, I
had not gone too far astray, I realize today is right and
yesterday was not.

—Tao Yuanming (365 – 427), poet of the Jin Dynasty

Terms:

a. 諫：補救 to remedy

b. 追：來得及做好 there is time to do better

5. 迷而知反，失道不遠。　　　—— 《三國志・魏書・王郎傳》

If you return in time from the wrong way, you won't
get too far astray.

*—History of the Three Kingdoms by Chen Shou
(233 – 297), historian of the Western Jin Dynasty*

6. 不遷怒，不貳過。　　　　　—— 《論語・雍也》

Never take your anger out on anyone else, and never
make the same mistake a second time.

*—The Analects, a Confucian classic recording
the words and deeds of Confucius and his dialogues with his disciples*

Terms:

a. 遷：轉移 to take out on

b. 貳：重複；犯同樣的錯誤 to make the same mistake a second time

7. 君子見善則遷，有過則改。　　——《周易·益·象》

When an honourable man finds that someone has performed a good conduct, he tries to learn from him (or he tries to do the same); when he makes any mistakes, he corrects him.

—The Book of Changes, a Confucian classic

Terms:

見善：看見別人行善 to have seen somebody perform a good conduct (or do a good thing)

8. 過日聞而德日新。　　——唐·白居易《策林四·納諫》

Have your mistakes pointed out every day and every day you can raise your moral integrity to a new standard.

—Bai Juyi (772 – 846), poet of the Tang Dynasty

Terms:

a. 過：過錯 mistakes
b. 日：每日 everyday
c. 聞：聽見 to hear
d. 新：達到新的境界 to a new standard

9. 君子之過，如日月之食焉：過也，人皆見之；
更也，人皆仰之。　　——《論語·子張》

An honourable man's mistake is like the eclipse of the sun or the moon: when he makes a mistake, it is witnessed by the public; when he corrects it, he is looked up to by the public.

*—The Analects, a Confucian classic recording
the words and deeds of Confucius and his dialogues with his disciples*

Terms:

a. 日月之食：日食和月食 eclipse of the sun or the moon

b. 更：改正 when the mistakes are corrected

c. 仰：仰慕 to look up to

10. 志不求易，事不避難。　　　——《後漢書‧虞詡列傳》

When you set your mind to a goal, do not go for what is easy; when you decide to take a task, do not dodge what is difficult.

—History of Eastern Han by Fan Ye (398 – 445), historian
of the State of Song of the Southern Dynasties

11. 欲窮千里目，更上一層樓。　——唐‧王之渙《登鸛雀樓》

1) If you want to see one thousand *li* away, you need to take one more storey.

2) For a better view further afield, go one more storey up.

—Wang Zhihuan (688 – 742), poet of the Tang Dynasty

Terms:

a. 窮：窮盡；（看）到頭 to see the farthest end

b. 更上一層樓：再上一層樓 one more storey up

12. 誰道人生無再少？門前流水尚能西，
休將白髮唱黃雞。　　　　——宋‧蘇軾《浣溪沙》

Who says life cannot become young again?
Even the river in front of the temple is flowing west.
There is no need to sigh that time goes fast and man
　　becomes old quickly.

—Su Shi (1037 – 1101), alias Su Dongpo,
poet of the Northern Song Dynasty

Terms:

少：年少 young in age

Notes:

a. 門前流水尚能西

As all the long rivers in China flow from west to east, people believe that it is impossible for any river to flow from east to west. When Su Shi (1037 –1101), the great poet of the Northern Song Dynasty, visited the Qingquan Temple in Qishui and saw the Lanxi River in front of it flowing west, he drew an analogy between the river and life. If the river could flow west, the aged could become young again. This shows Su Shi's optimism about life.

b. 休將白髮唱黃雞

This is an allusion to a poem by Bai Juyi in which the poet makes a metaphorical use of the squawks of a rooster in the morning as an indicator of quickly passing time, thus the association of grey hair with the yellow rooster.

（九）勇敢頑強
Be Courageous and Steadfast

1.　說大人則藐之，勿視其巍巍然。　　——《孟子・盡心下》

When you advise a prince, look down upon him and don't be scared by his commanding eminence.

—Mencius by Meng Ke (c.372 – 289 BC), philosopher
and Confucian scholar of the Warring States Period

Terms:

a. 說（shuì）：勸說 to persuade
b. 大人：這裏指諸侯 duke; prince

2.　不吐剛以茹柔，不附上以急下。　　——唐・白居易

Spit nothing hard and swallow nothing soft; do not

ingratiate yourself with your superior and do not
embarrass / coerce your inferior.

—Bai Juyi (772 – 846), poet of the Tang Dynasty

Terms:
a. 茹：吞 to swallow
b. 附上：附和上級 to ingratiate yourself with your superior
c. 急下：使下級窘迫；逼迫下級 to embarrass / coerce your inferior

3.   行曲，則違於臧獲；行直，則怒於諸侯。

——《韓非子・顯學》

If your conduct is unjustifiable, you can give in even
to a slave; if your conduct is justifiable, you can even
stand up to rebuke the prince.

—Hanfeizi by Han Fei (c.280 – 233 BC), legalist
and statesman of late Warring States Period

Terms:
a. 行曲：行為不合理 unreasonable conduct; unjustifiable conduct
b. 違：退讓 to give in to
c. 臧（zāng）獲：古代稱奴隸為臧獲 slaves
d. 行直：行為正當合理 reasonable conduct
e. 怒：怒斥 to rebuke

4.   天下有大勇者，卒然臨之而不驚，無故加之而不怒。

—— 宋・蘇軾《留侯論》

There are people of such great moral courage that
when disasters suddenly befall them, they are not
scared, and when they are humiliated for no reasons
whatsoever, they are not angry.

—Su Shi (1037 – 1101), alias Su Dongpo,
poet of the Northern Song Dynasty

Terms:

a. 卒（cù）：通"猝"，突然 suddenly
b. 臨：降臨 to befall
c. 加：施加 to impose upon

5. 林暗草驚風，將軍夜引弓。
　 平明尋白羽，沒在石棱中。　　　—— 唐 · 盧綸《塞下曲》

Night wind was rustling the grass in the forest,
The general bent his bow and shot into the darkness.
When looking for the arrow at dawn,
He found it had gone deep into a stone.

—Lu Lun (748 – 800), poet of the Tang Dynasty

Note:

The poem is based on a true story. Once Li Guang (? – 119 BC), a renowned general of the Western Han Dynasty, went hunting and mistook a rock in the grass for a tiger.

二、處世
Get along with People

(一) 謹慎
Be Prudent

1. 慎於言者不嘩，慎於行者不伐。 　　——《韓詩外傳》卷三

Those who are careful of their words are not
pretentious; those who are careful of their deeds are
not self-praising.

　　—Collections of Comments on Ancient Affairs with quotes from
　　The Book of Songs by Han Ying of the Western Han Dynasty

Terms:
a. 嘩：浮誇造作 pretentious
b. 伐：自我誇耀 to praise oneself

2. 君子欲訥於言而敏於行。 　　——《論語‧里仁》

An honourable man weighs his words before he
speaks, but he is quick in action.

　　—The Analects, a Confucian classic recording
　　the words and deeds of Confucius and his dialogues with his disciples

Terms:
a. 訥（nè）：出言遲緩；謹慎 to weigh one's words before he speaks
b. 敏：敏捷 quick

3. 輕諾必寡信，多易必多難。　——《老子·道德經六十三》

1) Light promises make one less trustworthy; he who takes things with ease will end up in difficulty.
2) Light promises make one's trustworthiness suffer; he who takes things casually will end up in difficulty.

　　　—Laozi by Li Er (李耳), philosopher of late Spring and Autumn Period, and founder of Taoism

Terms:
a. 輕諾：輕易許諾；隨便許諾 to make light promises
b. 寡信：難以守信 hard to keep your promises
c. 易：把事情看得容易 to take things with ease

4. 行必先人，言必後人。　——《大戴禮記·曾子立事》

1) Act ahead of others and speak after others.
2) Be the first to act and the last to speak.

　　　—Da Dai's Book of Rites compiled by Dai De, scholar on rites of the Western Han Dynasty

Terms:
a 行：做事 to act; to do things
b 先人：先於別人 before others

5. 可與言而不與之言，失人；不可與之言而與之言，失言。知者不失人，亦不言。　——《論語·衛靈公》

If you don't converse with a person who is worth conversing with, you lose the person; if you converse with a person who is not worth conversing with, you waste your words. A sensible man neither loses the person nor wastes his words.

　　　—The Analects, a Confucian classic recording the words and deeds of Confucius and his dialogues with his disciples

Terms:

a. 失人：失去可與之交往的人 to lose the person you can get along with

b. 失言：説了廢話 to waste your words

c. 知：通 "智"，聰明 sensible; wise

6. 白圭之玷，尚可磨也；斯言之玷，不可為也。

——《詩經・大雅・抑》

Spots on white jade can be ground off, but indiscreet remarks cannot be made up for.

—*The Book of Songs, China's first collection of ancient poems*

Terms:

a. 白圭（guī）：白色玉器 white jadeware

b. 玷（diàn）：白玉上的斑點 spots on white jade

c. 為：做，這裏是 "補救" 之意 to make up for; to remedy

7. 出其言善，則千里之外應之；……出其言不善，則千里之外違之。   ——《周易・繫辭上》

When a remark is made with well-meant intent, it is responded with approval a thousand *li* away; when a remark is made with wicked intent, it is opposed a thousand *li* away.

—*The Book of Changes, a Confucian classic*

Terms:

a. 應：贊同 to respond with approval

b. 違：反對 to oppose; to be opposed

8. 附耳之語，流聞千里。   ——《文子・微明》

A confidential whisper can travel a thousand *li* away.

—*Wenzi, a Taoist work by unknown*
author of the Warring States Period

Terms:
a. 附耳：貼近耳朵，意 "耳語" whispers
b. 流聞：流傳 to travel

9. 言而當，知也；默而當，亦知也。

——《荀子·非十二子》

It is wise to speak when speech is called for; it is also wise to keep silent when silence is called for.

—Xunzi by Xun Kuang (313 – 238 BC), thinker and educator of the Warring States Period

Terms:
a. 當：恰當；得體 appropriate
b. 知：通 "智"，有智慧 sensible; wise

10. 小人溺於水，君子溺於口，大人溺於民。

——《禮記·緇衣》

The ordinary people are drowned by water, scholar officials are drowned by words, and princes are drowned by the people they rule.

—The Book of Rites, a Confucian classic

Terms:
a. 小人：普通百姓 the ordinary people
b. 溺：被淹死 to be drowned
c. 大人：官員 government officials

11. 君子力如牛，不與牛爭力；走如馬，不與馬爭走；知如士，不與士爭知。 ——《荀子·堯問》

An honourable man is as strong as an ox, but he does not contend with an ox for strength; an honourable man is as fast as a horse, but he does not contend with a horse for speed; an honourable man is as intelligent as a *shi*, but he does not contend with a *shi* for intelligence.

—Xunzi by Xun Kuang (313 – 238 BC), thinker
and educator of the Warring States Period

Terms:

a. 爭：比高低 to contend with
b. 走：跑 to run
c. 知：智慧 intelligence

12. 君子不失足於人，不失色於人，不失口於人。

——《禮記‧表記》

An honourable man does not fail to behave with decorum, or look with demeanor, or speak with appropriateness.

—The Book of Rites, a Confucian classic

Terms:

a. 失足：舉止不莊重 to behave without decorum
b. 失色：表情不嚴肅 to look without demeanor
c. 失口：言語不當 to speak without appropriateness

13. 動莫若敬，居莫若儉，德莫若讓，事莫若諮。

——《國語‧周語下》

It's better to act with respect, practice thrift in everyday life, cultivate politeness and modesty, and breed the habit of consulting others in dealing with business.

—Remarks of Monarchs, history of late Western Zhou Dynasty
and other major states in the Spring and Autumn Period,
attributed to Zuo Qiuming, historian of the State of Lu

Terms:

a. 敬：尊敬別人 to respect others
b. 居：日常；平時 in everyday life
c. 讓：謙讓 be polite and modest
d. 諮：諮詢 to consult

14. 無功之賞，不義之富，禍之媒也。
　　　　　　　　　　　　　　——《晏子春秋・內篇・雜下》

Rewards received for no credit and riches amassed by dishonest means are both causes for misfortunes (or will lead to disasters).

—Yanzi's Spring and Autumn Annals, supposedly written by Yan Ying (? –500 BC), minister of the State of Qi during the Spring and Autumn Period

Terms:

a. 無功之賞：沒有功勞而接受獎賞 to receive a reward for no credit
b. 不義之富：通過不道德手段累積財富 to become rich by dishonest means
c. 媒：媒介；原因 causes for; to lead to

15. 美成在久，惡成不及改。　　——《莊子・人間世》

A good thing takes a long time to accomplish, but a bad thing can get done so quickly that you are left with no time to correct / regret.

—Zhuangzi by Zhuang Zhou (c.369 – 286 BC) and his followers of the Warring States Period

Terms:

a. 美：美好的事情 good things
b. 惡：壞事 bad things
c. 不及改：來不及改正；後悔莫及 with no time to correct / regret

16. 善游者溺，善騎者墮。　　　　　　　——《文子‧符言》

Good swimmers tend to get drowned, and good riders
tend to fall from horseback.

—Wenzi, a Taoist work by unknown
author of the Warring States Period

17. 知不務多，務審其所知；言不務多，務審其所謂；
行不務多，務審其所由。　　　——《荀子‧哀公》

One does not have to know a lot, but he has to make
sure what he knows is correct; one does not have to
talk a lot, but he has to make sure what he talks about
is appropriate; one does not have to do a lot, but he
has to make sure what he does is justified.

—Xunzi by Xun Kuang (313 – 238 BC), thinker
and educator of the Warring States Period

Terms:
a. 不務：不必；不求 not have to; not to seek
b. 務審：一定要細究 to make sure
c. 所知：所知是否正確 whether what one knows is correct
d. 所謂：所說是否恰當 whether what one says is appropriate
e. 所由：所做是否正當 whether what one does is justified

18. 非禮勿視，非禮勿聽，非禮勿言，非禮勿動。

——《論語‧顏淵》

Do not look at anything that is not in conformity
with the rituals; do not listen to anything that is
not in conformity with the rituals; do not talk about
anything that is not in conformity with the rituals;
and do not do anything that is not in conformity with
the rituals.

—The Analects, a Confucian classic recording
the words and deeds of Confucius and his dialogues with his disciples

Terms:
禮：禮儀，古代奴隸主貴族的道德規範 rituals evolved and observed by ancient aristocrats

19. 君子有終身之憂，無一朝之患。　——《孟子·離婁下》

An honourable man is alert all his life to the possibility of making mistakes, so that he has no unexpected calamities.

— Mencius by Meng Ke (c. 372 – 289 BC), philosopher and Confucian scholar of the Warring States Period

Terms:
a. 終身：一生 all one's life
b. 一朝：一天 for a single day

20. 勤力可以不貧，謹身可以避禍。

——北朝·北魏·賈思勰《齊民要術》

Diligence can make one free from poverty, and prudence can make one free from calamities.

— Important Arts for the People's Welfare by Jia Sixie, agronomist of the Northern Wei Dynasty (386 – 534)

21. 君子安其身而後動，易其心而後語，定其交而後求。

——《周易·繫辭下》

An honourable man should stand firm first and then act, be composed first and then speak, make bosom friends first and then ask for help.

— The Book of Changes, a Confucian classic

Terms:
a. 安其身：使身體站穩 to stand firm
b. 易其心：使心地平和 to be composed
c. 定其交：與人有深交 to make bosom friends

（二） 名利富貴
Be Indifferent to Fame and Fortune

1. 舉世而譽之而不加勸，舉世而非之而不加沮。

——《莊子・逍遙遊》

Acclaimed by the whole country, he is not encouraged;
condemned by the whole country, he is not discouraged.

—*Zhuangzi by Zhuang Zhou (c.369 – 286 BC)*
and his followers of the Warring States Period

Terms:
a. 舉世：全國 the whole country; people of the whole country
b. 加勸：受到鼓舞 be encouraged
c. 沮（jǔ）：灰心 be discouraged

2. 抱真才者，人不知不慍。

—— 明・王文祿《海沂子・真才論》

When a learned and talented person is not understood
by others, he is not irritated.

—*Wang Wenlu of the Ming Dynasty*

Terms:
a. 抱真才者：有真才實學的人 learned and talented people
b. 慍：惱怒 angry; irritated

3. 聞毀勿戚戚，聞譽勿欣欣，自顧行何如，毀譽安足論。

—— 唐・白居易《續座右銘》

When you are slandered, don't be sad; when you
are extolled, don't be elated. What you need to do
is examine yourself on your moral integrity. Either
slandered or extolled, that is not anything to speak of.

—*Bai Juyi (772 – 846), poet of the Tang Dynasty*

Terms:
a. 戚戚：悲傷 sad
b. 欣欣：高興 glad; extolled
c. 自顧行何如：看看自己的品行如何 just examine yourself on your moral integrity
d. 毀譽安足論：毀謗也好，讚美也好，都不值得考慮 either slandered or extolled, that is not anything to speak of

4.   至樂無樂，至譽無譽。   ——《莊子・至樂》

True joy is not mixed with worldly joys; true honour is not mixed with worldly honours.

—Zhuangzi by Zhuang Zhou (c.369 – 286 BC)
and his followers of the Warring States Period

Terms:
a. 至樂：極樂 true joy
b. 至譽：最大的榮譽 true honour

5.   與其有譽於前，孰若無毀於其後；與其有樂於身，孰若無憂於其心。

—— 唐・韓愈《送李願歸盤谷序》

Better not to be slandered after death than praised while alive; better not to have mental worries than enjoy material luxuries.

—Han Yu (768 – 824), writer and philosopher of the Tang Dynasty

Terms:
a. 前：生前 while alive
b. 後：死後 after death

6. 君子禍至不懼，福至不喜。   ——《史記・孔子世家》

A man of moral integrity is not scared by calamities, nor is he elated at good fortunes.

*—Historical Records by Sima Qian (c.145
or 135 – ? BC) of the Han Dynasty*

Terms:

君子：a man of moral integrity = an honourable man

7. 功名畫地餅，歲月下江船。

——宋・周孚《元日懷陳道人並憶焦山舊遊》

The official position one seeks is like a cake drawn on the ground, and the years one passes are like a boat gliding down the river.

—Zhou Fu (1135 – 1177) of the Southern Song Dynasty

8. 不榮通，不醜窮。   ——《莊子・天地》

1) Do not take your success as anything honourable, and do not take your poverty as anything ugly.
2) Do not take it as anything honourable just because you are successful in life, and do not take it as anything repulsive just because you are poverty-stricken.

*—Zhuangzi by Zhuang Zhou (c.369 – 286 BC)
and his followers of the Warring States Period*

Terms:

a. 榮：以……為榮 to take something as honourable
b. 通：得志 be successful in life and career
c. 醜：醜陋 to take something as ugly / repulsive

9. 不立異以為高，不逆情以干譽。

—— 宋・歐陽修《縱囚論》

Don't try to be unconventional in order to show off as a smart aleck, and don't go against common sense in order to achieve fame.

—Ouyang Xiu (1007 – 1072), writer and
poet of the Northern Song Dynasty

Terms:
a. 立異：做不合常情之事 be unconventional
b. 逆情：違背常情 against common sense
c. 干譽：追求好名聲 to achieve fame

10. 有一片凍不死衣，有一口餓不死食，貧無煩惱知閑貴。

—— 元・馬致遠《般涉調・哨遍》

With a piece of rags to wear, I won't be frozen to death; with a mouthful of food to eat, I won't be starved to death. So, being a poor man, I have no worries, and appreciate being leisurely and carefree.

— Ma Zhiyuan (c.1250 – c.1324),
playwright of the Yuan Dynasty

Terms:
a. 有一片凍不死衣：有一片衣服，我凍不死 with a piece of rags to wear, I won't be frozen to death
b. 有一口餓不死食：有一口飯吃，我餓不死 with a mouthful of food to eat, I won't be starved to death

11. 為富不仁矣，為仁不富矣。　　——《孟子・滕文公上》

Those who seek wealth are not humane; those who devote themselves to humaneness are not wealthy.

—Mencius by Meng Ke (c.372 – 289 BC), philosopher
and Confucian scholar of the Warring States Period

Terms:

a. 為：追求 to seek; to go for

b. 富：富有 be rich

12. 人生何謂富？山水繞吾廬。
　　人生何謂貴？閉戶讀我書。

—— 清·汪應銓《題讀書樓》

What is wealth? To live in a house with mountains
　　and rivers around.
What is dignity? To read my books behind closed doors.

—*Wang Yingquan (1685 – 1745) of the Qing Dynasty*

Terms:

a. 廬：房子 house

b. 閉戶：關門 with doors closed

13. 古之所謂得志者，非軒冕之謂也。　——《莊子·繕性》

In ancient times what makes people pleased was not
high-ranking positions.

—*Zhuangzi by Zhuang Zhou (c. 369 – 286 BC)*
and his followers of the Warring States Period

Terms:

a. 得志：得意 to be pleased

b. 軒冕：卿大夫所坐的車子和所戴的禮帽，這裏指高官顯位
carriages and hats used by scholar officials, referring to high-
ranking positions

14. 榮進之心日頹，任實之情轉篤。

　　　　　　　　——三國・魏・嵇康《與山巨源絕交書》

Day by day, my idea of assuming office is declining,
and my mind is becoming more and more practical.

—Ji Kang (224 – 263), writer, thinker and musician
of the State of Wei of the Three Kingdoms

Terms:

a. 榮進：指做官 to seek an official position
b. 頹：衰退 to decline
c. 任實：講求實際 be practical
d. 篤：加重 be more inclined

15. 君子辭貴不辭賤，辭富不辭貧。　　——《禮記・坊記》

An honourable man can abandon a high ranking
position, but he does not care about his humble
situation; he can abandon riches, but he does not care
about poverty.

—The Book of Rites, a Confucian classic

（三）自強自立
Be Self-supporting

1. 鑒明，則塵垢不止。　　　　　——《莊子・德充符》

When the mirror is well cleaned, it doesn't gather dust
on it.

—Zhuangzi by Zhuang Zhou (c.369 – 286 BC)
and his followers of the Warring States Period

Terms:

鑒：鏡子 mirror

2. 以人言善我，必以人言罪我。　　——《韓非子・説林上》

If you think good of me because someone says something in my favour, you are sure to condemn me when someone says anything against me.

—Hanfeizi by Han Fei (c.280 – 233 BC), legalist
and statesman of late Warring States Period

Terms:
a. 以：因為 because
b. 善：認為……好 to think good of
c. 罪：怪罪 to condemn

3. 恃人不如自恃也；人之為己者，不如己之自為也。

——《韓非子・外儲説右下》

1) Rely on yourself rather than on others; do it by yourself rather than ask others to do it for you.

2) To rely on others is not as safe as on yourself; to ask others to do it for you is not as secure as to do it by yourself.

—Hanfeizi by Han Fei (c.280 – 233 BC), legalist
and statesman of late Warring States Period

Terms:
a. 恃 (shì)：依賴；靠 to rely on
b. 人之為 (wèi) 己者：讓別人為自己做事 to ask others to do it for you
c. 自為 (wéi)：自己做 to do it by yourself

4. 當為秋霜，無為檻羊。　　——《後漢書・光武十王列傳》

Be the conquering autumnal frost instead of lambs penned in the fold.

—History of Eastern Han by Fan Ye (398 – 445),
historian of the State of Song of the Southern Dynasties

Terms:

a. 當：應當 be; should be
b. 無：通"毋"，不要 be not; don't
c. 檻羊：羊圈裏的羊 lambs in the fold

5. 　不隨俗而雷同，不逐聲而寄論。

——漢·王符《潛夫論·交際》

Do not drift along with prevalent opinions and echo what others say, nor hang on others' views and indulge in empty talk.

—Social Evils through the Eye of a Hermit by Wang Fu (c.85 – 162), philosopher of the Eastern Han Dynasty

Terms:

a. 隨俗：附和世俗之見 to drift along with prevalent opinions
b. 雷同：人云亦云 to echo what others say
c. 逐聲：隨聲 to hang on others' views
d. 寄論：高談闊論 to indulge in empty talk

（四）獨善其身
Be Self-edifying

1. 　窮則獨善其身，達則兼善天下。　　——《孟子·盡心上》

When you are under adverse circumstances, cultivate your mind and breed your moral integrity; when you are successful in life, devote yourself to helping the country.

—Mencius by Meng Ke (c.372 – 289 BC), philosopher and Confucian scholar of the Warring States Period

Terms:
a. 窮：困厄 be under adverse circumstances
b. 達：得志 be successful in life

2. 時來則來，時往則往。 ——漢・揚雄《法言・問明》

When it's time to come, come; when it's time to go, go.

*—Yang Xiong (53 BC – 18 AD), writer and
philosopher of the Western Han Dynasty*

Comment: It's important to understand the times and know what is the appropriate thing to do under certain circumstances.

3. 可以速而速，可以久而久，可以處而處，可以仕而仕。

——《孟子・萬章下》

When you are required to quit, quit; when you are required to stay, stay; when you are required to seclude, seclude; when you are required to take office, take it.

*—Mencius by Meng Ke (c.372 – 289 BC), philosopher
and Confucian scholar of the Warring States Period*

Terms:
a. 速：離開 to quit
b. 久：久留 to stay
c. 處：獨處 to seclude oneself
d. 仕：做官 to undertake office

4. 秋蛇向穴，不失其節。 ——漢・焦贛《焦氏易林》

In autumn, snakes will go to their caves; they never miss the season.

—Jiao Gong of the Han Dynasty

Terms:

節：節氣 season

Comment: Snakes change their habits with the change of seasons. Man should also adapt themselves to circumstances.

（五）隨遇而安
Adapt Oneself to Circumstances

1. 敬之而不喜，侮之而不怒。 ——《莊子‧庚桑楚》

1) He is not transported with joy when esteemed, nor is he transported with anger when humiliated.
2) Esteem doesn't make him happy, and humiliation doesn't make him angry.

—Zhuangzi by Zhuang Zhou (c.369 – 286 BC) and his followers of the Warring States Period

2. 處小而不逼，處大而不窕。 ——《淮南子‧原道訓》

In a small place, you don't feel it's crowded; in a big place, you don't feel it's spacious.

—Huainanzi by Prince Huainan Liu An (179 – 122 BC) and some of his followers of the Western Han Dynasty

Terms:

a. 逼：狹窄 crowded; cramped
b. 窕（tiǎo）：寬敞 spacious

3. 泰山不要欺毫末，顏子無心羨老彭。

——唐‧白居易《放言》五首其五

Mount Tai should not look down upon small things; Yan Hui has no mind to look up to Lao Peng.

—Bai Juyi (772 – 846), poet of the Tang Dynasty

Terms:

a. 泰山：具有象徵意義的高山，位於山東省 a mountain in Shandong Province, symbolic of significant things

b. 毫末：毫髮的尖端，喻微小之物 tip of the hair, a metaphor for small things

c. 顏子：顏回 one of Confucius favourite disciples who died young

d. 老彭：彭祖 a legendary figure who lived to be 800 years old

4. 釣罷歸來不繫船，江村月落正堪眠。
縱然一夜風吹去，只在蘆花淺水邊。

—— 唐・司空曙《江村即事》

Back from angling, I left the boat untied,
With the moon sliding down behind the village,
It's good time to go to sleep.
Even if the boat was blown away by night wind,
It could only land in the shallow water by the
    blooming reeds.

—Sikong Shu (c.720 – c.790), poet of the Tang Dynasty

Comment: This poem shows the poet's carefree lifestyle and his subtle state of mind.

5. 窮亦樂，通亦樂。   ——《莊子・讓王》

1) Stay happy under adverse circumstances, and stay happy under favourable circumstances.

2) Be happy under adverse circumstances as well as under favourable circumstances.

—Zhuangzi by Zhuang Zhou (c.369 – 286 BC)
and his followers of the Warring States Period

Terms:

a. 窮：境況不順利的時候 under adverse circumstances

b. 通：境況順利的時候 under favourable circumstances

6. 呼我牛也而謂之牛，呼我馬也而謂之馬。

——《莊子・天道》

Call me cow and my name is cow; call me horse and my name is horse.

—Zhuangzi by Zhuang Zhou (c.369 – 286 BC)
and his followers of the Warring States Period

Note:

Laozi believes that when you are censured, the censure itself causes pain, and if you do not accept the censure, the pain will aggravate. So it's better to live with whatever you are called.

（六）淡泊
Be Nonchalant to Worldly Concerns

1. 不恬不愉，非德也。　　　　——《莊子・在宥》

Be (or keep yourself) free from desires for fame and fortune, and be (or keep yourself) pleased with circumstances, otherwise it is inconsistent with human nature.

—Zhuangzi by Zhuang Zhou (c.369 – 286 BC)
and his followers of the Warring States Period

Terms:
a. 恬：淡泊寧靜 to keep aloof from desire for fame and fortune
b. 愉：和悅自適 be pleased with circumstances
c. 德：本性 human nature

2. 勝人者有力，自勝者強。　　——《老子・道經三十三》

He who conquers others is powerful; he who conquers himself is a strong character.

—Laozi by Li Er (李耳 *), philosopher of late Spring*
and Autumn Period, and founder of Taoism

3. 寂寂寥寥揚子居，年年歲歲一牀書。
獨有南山桂花發，飛來飛去襲人裾。

—— 唐·盧照鄰《長安古意》

Lonely, solitary, I live in a cottage as simple as Yang
　　Xiong's home.
Year in, year out, I keep company with my books
　　filling up the shelf.
Only when the osmanthus flowers blossom on the
　　South Mountain,
Their aromatic fragrance comes along, drifting into
　　my bosom.

—Lu Zhaolin (c.635 – c.689), poet of early Tang Dynasty

Terms:

a. 寂寂寥寥：寂靜，冷落 lonely; solitary
b. 揚子居：揚雄的住宅 the home of Yang Xiong (53 BC – 18
　 AD), writer and philosopher of the Western Han Dynasty
c. 南山：終南山，在今陝西省 Zhongnan Mountain in Shaanxi
　 Province
d. 裾：衣襟，指胸懷 bosom

4. 善生者必善死。　　　　　　—— 明·莊元臣《叔苴子》

He who knows how to live his life will die a good
death.

—Zhuang Yuanchen (1560 – 1609) of the Ming Dynasty

5. 其寢不夢，其覺無憂。　　　　　—— 《莊子·大宗師》

He sleeps with no dreams and awakens with no worries.

—Zhuangzi by Zhuang Zhou (c.369 – 286 BC)
and his followers of the Warring States Period

Terms:

a. 寢（qǐn）：睡覺 to sleep; be asleep
b. 夢：做夢 to dream
c. 覺：醒來 to awaken; be awake

6. 逢人不説人間事，便是人間無事人。

——唐‧杜荀鶴《贈質上人》

He who does not talk about worldly affairs is one who is free from worldly concerns.

—Du Xunhe (846 – 904), poet of the Tang Dynasty

（七）韜光養晦
Keep a Low Profile

1. 蟄伏於盛夏，藏華於當春。　　　——《抱朴子‧嘉遁》

Hibernate in midsummer, and keep from blooming in spring.

—Baopuzi by Ge Hong (284 – 364) of the East Jin Dynasty

Terms:

a. 蟄伏：指蛇獸類動物冬天長眠於洞穴之中 snakes and animals hibernate in caves in winter
b. 藏華：不開花 to keep from blooming

Note:

This has the same connotation as 韜光養晦, keeping a low profile.

2. 知淵中之魚者不祥。　　　——《韓非子‧説林上》

He who can sense fish in deep water will end up in dire fortune.

—Hanfeizi by Han Fei (c.280 – 233 BC), legalist
and statesman of late Warring States Period

Terms:

a. 淵：深水 deep water

b. 祥：吉利 auspicious

Note:

If one is too smart in mind reading, he will come to no good end.

3.　我必先之，彼故知之；我必賣之，彼故鬻之。

──《莊子‧徐無鬼》

I must have shown off my capabilities first and then
they get to know about them; I must have meant to
trade my capabilities and then they want to buy them.

—Zhuangzi by Zhuang Zhou (c.369 – 286 BC)
and his followers of the Warring States Period

Terms:

a. 先之：先表現出來有才能 to show off your capabilities first

b. 鬻（yù）：買 to buy

4.　大勇若怯，大智若愚。　── 宋‧蘇軾《賀歐陽少師致仕啟》

1) People of great courage look timid; people of great
   wisdom look unintelligent.

2) Great courage looks like timidity; great wisdom
   looks like unintelligence.

—Su Shi (1037 – 1101), alias Su Dongpo,
poet of the Northern Song Dynasty

Terms:

怯（qiè）：膽小 timid

5. 白璧不可為，容容多後福。　　——《後漢書·左雄列傳》

It doesn't work trying to create a noble and unsullied image of yourself like white jade, but it will bring you good fortune to remain harmonious with other people.

—History of Eastern Han by Fan Ye (398 – 445), historian
of the State of Song of the Southern Dynasties

Terms:
a. 白璧：白玉 white jade, a metaphor for people of noble and unsullied character
b. 容容：融洽；和諧 be harmonious

6. 甘井近竭，招木近伐。　　——《墨子·親士》

Wells of sweet water get dried up, and tall trees get felled.

— Mozi, complete works of the Mohist school of
thought founded by Mo Di (c.468 – 376 BC)

Terms:
a. 甘：甜 sweet
b. 竭：枯竭 be dried up
c. 招木：大樹 tall trees
d. 伐：砍伐 to fell trees

7. 山抱玉，則鑿之；江懷珠，則竭之；豹配文，則剝之；人含智，則嫉之。　　——北齊·劉晝《劉子·言苑》

Mountains with jade in them get dug up; rivers with pearls in them get dried up; leopards with spots on them get skinned; people with wisdom get begrudged.

—Liuzi by Liu Zhou (514 – 565), writer of the Northern Qi Dynasty

Terms:
a. 珠：珍珠 pearls
b. 文：斑點 spots

8.　俗人昭昭，我獨昏昏。　　　——《老子・道經二十》

Worldly people tend to boast about themselves, while
I alone like to keep a low profile.

> —*Laozi by Li Er (李耳), philosopher of late Spring*
> *and Autumn Period, and founder of Taoism*

Terms:

a. 昭昭：光彩照人，此處指自我誇耀 brilliant, meaning self-praise
b. 昏昏：不露光彩，此處指不顯示自己 to keep a low profile

9.　鳥獸不厭高，魚鱉不厭深。　　　——《莊子・庚桑楚》

1) For birds, the higher they fly, the better; for fish,
   the deeper they swim, the better.
2) Birds are never satisfied with the height of the sky
   and fish are never satisfied with the depth of the
   water.

> —*Zhuangzi by Zhuang Zhou (c.369 – 286 BC)*
> *and his followers of the Warring States Period*

Terms:

a. 鳥獸：主要指鳥 birds
b. 厭：滿足 be satisfied

10.　水流下，不爭疾，故去而不遲。　　　——《文子・符言》

As water flows toward low places with no intent to
vie for speed, it is not slow.

> —*Wenzi, a Taoist work by unknown*
> *author of the Warring States Period*

Terms:

a. 不爭疾：不爭快慢 not to vie for speed
b. 不遲：不慢 not slow

（八）隱居歸田
Pastoral Life

1. 日出而作，日入而息。 ——《慎子·外篇》

Go to work when the sun rises, and come back to rest when the sun sets.

— *Shenzi by Shen Dao of the Warring States Period*

Comment: This reflects the lifestyle of the people in primitive times.

2. 山中何所有？嶺上多白雲。
只可自怡悅，不堪持贈君。

——南朝·梁·陶弘景《詔問山中何所有賦詩以答》

What is there up in the mountain?
White clouds floating over its peak.
This I can appreciate by myself only,
But I cannot give it to you as a gift.

—*Tao Hongjing (456 – 536), Taoist thinker of the State of Liang of the Southern Dynasties*

3. 松下問童子，言師採藥去。
只在此山中，雲深不知處。 ——唐·賈島《尋隱者不遇》

Where is your master, I ask the lad.
He is off to pick herbs, the lad says,
Somewhere in the mountain, anyway,
but, as the clouds are thick and fog heavy,
I don't know where he is, exactly.

—*Jia Dao (779 – 843), poet of the Tang Dynasty*

4. 功成不受爵，長揖歸田廬。   ── 晉・左思《詠史》

I have done my share of the service, but I won't take any official post assigned to me. Farewell, I am going to settle back in the country.

—Zuo Si (c.250 – c.305), writer of the Western Jin Dynasty

Terms:

a. 爵：爵位 official post offered by the monarch
b. 揖：作揖 a traditional way of saluting by making a deep bow with both hands folded in front
c. 田廬：鄉下的家 home in the country

（九）待人
Treating People the Right Way

1. 物有不可忘，或有不可不忘。   ──《史記・魏公子列傳》

There are things that you should not forget, and there are things that you must forget.

—Historical Records by Sima Qian (c.145 or 135 – ? BC) of the Han Dynasty

Terms:
物：事物 things

Comment: Forget the good things you have done to others but don't forget the good things others have done to you.

2. 欲人之愛己也，必先愛人；欲人之從己也，必先從人。

——《國語·晉語四》

If you want to be loved, love others first; if you want to be obeyed, obey others first.

—Remarks of Monarchs, history of late Western Zhou Dynasty and other major states in the Spring and Autumn Period, attributed to Zuo Qiuming, historian of the State of Lu

3. 仁者以其所愛及其所不愛。　　——《孟子·盡心下》

The humane people extend their kindness for the ones they love to the ones they don't love.

—Mencius by Meng Ke (c.372 – 289 BC), philosopher and Confucian scholar of the Warring States Period

Terms:

a. 所愛：給予所愛的人的恩德 the kindness they give to the ones they love

b. 所不愛：不愛的人 the ones they do not love

c. 其：指"仁者" the humane people

4. 老吾老，以及人之老；幼吾幼，以及人之幼。

——《孟子·梁惠王上》

Show reverential respect to the aged of your own and extend the respect to the aged of others; cherish the children of your own and extend the love to the children of others.

—Mencius by Meng Ke (c.372 – 289 BC), philosopher and Confucian scholar of the Warring States Period

Terms:

a. 老：第一個"老"是形容詞用作動詞，意為對老年人敬重；第二、三個"老"是形容詞用作名詞，意為老年人 The first "老" is an adjective used as a verb, meaning to respect the aged; the second and third "老" are adjectives used as a noun, referring to the aged people.

b. 幼：第一個 "幼" 是形容詞用作動詞，意為對孩子愛護、撫養；第二、三個 "幼" 是形容詞用作名詞，意為孩子

The first "幼" is an adjective used as a verb, meaning to cherish and bring up children; the second and third "幼" are adjectives used as a noun, referring to the young children.

c. 及：推及；推廣 to extend

5. **己所不欲，勿施於人。**   ——《論語·衛靈公》

1) Do not do to others what you do not like yourself.

2) Do not do to others what you do not like to be done to yourself.

3) Do not impose upon others what you do not like yourself.

4) Do not impose upon others what you do not like to be imposed upon yourself.

> *—The Analects, a Confucian classic recording the words and*
> *deeds of Confucius and his dialogues with his disciples*

6. **己先則援之，彼先則推之。** ——《大戴禮記·曾子制言上》

When you get ahead of others, give a hand and pull them along with you; when others get ahead of you, give a hand and push them further ahead.

> *—Da Dai's Book of Rites compiled by Dai De,*
> *scholar on rites of the Western Han Dynasty*

Terms:

a. 援：拉 to pull

b. 彼：別人 others

7. 君子成人之美，不成人之惡。　　　——《論語‧顏淵》

An honourable man helps others to realize what they
do for a good purpose, but not what they do for an evil
purpose.

*—The Analects, a Confucian classic recording
the words and deeds of Confucius and his dialogues with his disciples*

Terms:
a. 成：成全 to help to realize
b. 美：好事 what is good
c. 惡：壞事 evil intent

8. 君子過人以為友，不及人以為師。

——《晏子春秋‧外篇》

When an honourable man outshines others, he takes
them as his friends; when he is outshone by others, he
respects them as his teachers.

*—Yanzi's Spring and Autumn Annals, supposedly written
by Yan Ying (? – 500 BC), minister of the State of Qi
during the Spring and Autumn Period*

Terms:
a. 過人：（品行、才能）超過別人 to outshine others; be better than
others
b. 不及：不如 to be outshone; not as good as others

9. 竭誠，則胡越為一體；傲物，則骨肉為行路。

—— 唐‧魏徵《諫太宗十思疏》

Honesty can bring the Hu and Yue nationalities
together; arrogance can make one's flesh and blood
like passers-by.

—Wei Zheng (580 – 643), statesman of the Tang Dynasty

Terms:

a. 胡：古代中國北方少數民族 a minority nationality living to the
   north of ancient China

b. 越：古代中國南方少數民族 a minority nationality living to the
   south of ancient China

c. 傲物：傲視他人 arrogance

d. 骨肉：親人 flesh and blood

e. 行路：路人 passers-by

10. 天下皆知取之為取，莫知與之為取。

——《後漢書‧桓譚列傳》

Everyone in the world knows how to take what they
want, but they do not know that they should give first
and then take.

*—History of Eastern Han by Fan Ye (398 – 445), historian
of the State of Song of the Southern Dynasties*

Terms:

a. 天下：天下人 people of the world

b. 莫知：不知 do not know

三、識人
Understand People in Perspective

（一）知賢
Distinguish People by Virtue and Talent

1. 以玉為石者，亦將以石為玉矣。　　——《抱朴子·擢才》

He who takes jade for rock will take rock for jade.

—Baopuzi by Ge Hong (284 – 364) of the East Jin Dynasty

Terms:

以⋯⋯為⋯⋯：to take something for something else

Comment: It is important to be able to tell the honest from the dishonest, the honourable from the dishonourable and the talented from the mediocre.

2. 愛而知其惡，憎而知其善。　　——《禮記·曲禮上》

When you like a person, you should know he has his weakness; when you dislike a person, you should know he has his merit.

—The Book of Rites, a Confucian classic

Terms:

a. 惡：缺點；短處 weakness
b. 善：優點；長處 merit

3. 知人則哲，能官人。 ——《尚書·皋陶謨》

He who understands people is wise, and a wise man can make the right appointments.

—Collection of Ancient Texts, a Confucian classic

Terms:

a. 哲：聰明 wise

b. 官：任用 to appoint somebody to the right position; to make the best use of people

4. 世有伯樂，然後有千里馬。千里馬常有，而伯樂不常有。 —— 唐·韓愈《雜説下》

There is Bo Le first and then there are winged steeds in the world. Winged steeds are not difficult to find, but Bo Le is.

—Han Yu (768 – 824), writer and
philosopher of the Tang Dynasty

Terms:

a. 千里馬：有才能者 a fast horse that can gallop one thousand *li* a day, a metaphor for capable people

b. 伯樂：古之善相馬者 a legendary person who is expert at judging horses; metaphorically, a person who can discover capable people

5. 人固不易知，知人亦未易也！ ——《史記·范雎蔡澤列傳》

Man is not easy to understand, ah, it is really not easy to understand a man!

—Historical Records by Sima Qian
(c.145 or 135 – ? BC) of the Han Dynasty

6. 是是非非謂之知，非是是非謂之愚。

——《荀子·修身》

To say "yes" to what is right and "no" to what is
wrong is judicious; to say "no" to what is right and
"yes" to what is wrong is absurd.

*—Xunzi by Xun Kuang (313 – 238 BC), thinker
and educator of the Warring States Period*

Terms:

a. 是是：肯定正確的東西。第一個"是"為動詞，"肯定"的意思；第二個"是"為名詞，"正確"的意思。The first "是" is a verb which says "yes" to the second "是" as a noun meaning what is correct.

b. 非非：否定錯誤的東西。第一個"非"是動詞，"否定"的意思；第二個"非"是名詞，"錯誤"的意思。The first "非" is a verb which says "no" to the second "非" as a noun meaning what is wrong.

c. 非是：否定正確的東西。非，動詞，"否定"的意思；是，名詞，"正確"的意思。"非" is a verb which says "no" to "是" as a noun meaning what is correct.

d. 是非：肯定錯誤的東西。是，動詞，"肯定"的意思；非，名詞，"錯誤"的意思。"是" is a verb which says "yes" to "非" as a noun meaning what is wrong.

7. 不患人之不己知，患不知人也。   ——《論語·學而》

One should not worry about being not understood, but
he should worry about not understanding others.

*—The Analects, a Confucian classic recording
the words and deeds of Confucius and his dialogues with his disciples*

Terms:

a. 患：擔心 to worry

b. 人不己知：別人不了解自己 not be understood

8. 知人者智，自知者明。   ——《老子・道經三十三》

He who understands others is intelligent but he who
understands himself is wise.

—Laozi by Li Er (李耳) *, philosopher of late Spring
and Autumn Period, and founder of Taoism*

Terms:
a. 智：聰明 clever; intelligent
b. 明：明達 sensible; wise

9. 馬之似鹿者千金，天下無千金之鹿。

——《淮南子・説山訓》

A horse that looks like deer is worth a thousand pieces
of gold, but there is no deer in the world worth that
much.

*—Huainanzi by Prince Huainan Liu An (179 – 122 BC)
and some of his followers of the Western Han Dynasty*

Comment: Commonplace things become valuable, when
associated with valuable things. This is sarcastic about those
who, instead of cherishing real good things, take commonplace
things as treasures.

10. 盜名不如盜貨。   ——《荀子・不苟》

A thief of prestige is even worse than a thief of property.

*—Xunzi by Xun Kuang (313 – 238 BC), thinker
and educator of the Warring States Period*

Terms:
a. 盜：偷盜 to steal
b. 名：名譽 fame; prestige
c. 貨：財物 property

11. 知者樂水，仁者樂山。 　　　　　　　　——《論語・雍也》

Wise people love rivers, and humane people love mountains.

—The Analects, a Confucian classic recording
the words and deeds of Confucius and his dialogues with his disciples

Terms:
a. 知：通 "智" wise; wisdom
b. 樂（yào）：喜愛 to love

12. 疾風知勁草之心，大雪見貞松之節。

——唐・白居易《與劉濟詔》

The unyielding tenacity of grass stands the test of swift winds and the unwavering spirit of the pine is witnessed in heavy snows.

—Bai Juyi (772 – 846), poet of the Tang Dynasty

Terms:
a. 疾風：大風，迅猛的風 strong winds; swift winds
b. 貞：堅貞 unwavering spirit

13. 大寒既至，霜雪既降，吾是以知松柏之茂也。

——《莊子・讓王》

It is only when the bitter winter blows and snow and frost fall that I find the pines and cypresses tough and green with exuberance.

—Zhuangzi by Zhuang Zhou (c. 369 – 286 BC)
and his followers of the Warring States Period

Terms:
a. 是以：因此 therefore
b. 茂：生命力茂盛 (of plants) exuberant

14. 勁松彰於歲寒，貞臣見於國危。 —— 晉‧潘嶽《西征賦》

The toughness of the pine is exhibited in the severe cold of the winter and the loyalty of ministers is manifested in the crises of the country.

—Pan Yue (247 – 300), writer of the Western Jin Dynasty

Terms:
a. 彰：顯現 to exhibit
b. 見（xiàn）：出現 to be manifested

15. 道遠知驥，世偽知賢。 —— 三國‧魏‧曹植《矯志》

A good steed is tried out by distance and a virtuous man is distinguished when the moral standard of the day deteriorates.

*—Cao Zhi (192 – 232), poet of the
State of Wei of the Three Kingdoms*

Terms:
a. 驥：良馬 good steed
b. 賢：賢人 virtuous people

16. 試玉要燒三日滿，辨材須待七年期。

—— 唐‧白居易《放言》五首其三

1) Genuine jade can stand the test of fire for three full days and a tall tree is not distinguished until it's grown for seven years.
2) Genuine jade does not become hot after it's heated in fire for three full days and a tall tree cannot be distinguished until it has grown for seven years.

—Bai Juyi (772 – 846), poet of the Tang Dynasty

Terms:

a. 試玉：詩人自註："真玉燒三日不熱" The poet's note says "Genuine jade does not become hot when heated in fire for three days."

b. 辨材：詩人自註："豫章木生七年而後知" The poet's note says "You cannot tell whether it's a tall tree or not after it has grown for seven years."

Comment: It takes time to know a person.

17. 眾惡之，必察焉；眾好之，必察焉。

——《論語・衛靈公》

When a person is disliked by everyone, you must find out why; when a person is liked by everyone, you must find out why.

—The Analects, a Confucian classic recording the words and deeds of Confucius and his dialogues with his disciples

Terms:

a. 惡（wù）：憎惡 to dislike

b. 好（hào）：喜歡 to like

18. 巧詐不如拙誠。

——《韓非子・説林》

Be inept and sincere rather than deft and crafty.

—Hanfeizi by Han Fei (c.280 – 233 BC), legalist and statesman of late Warring States Period

19. 面譽者不忠，飾貌者不情。

——《大戴禮記・文王官人》

He who praises one in his presence is not loyal and he who puts on a show covers up the truth.

—Da Dai's Book of Rites compiled by Dai De, scholar on rites of the Western Han Dynasty

Terms:

a. 面：當面 in one's presence

b. 飾貌：裝模作樣 to put on a show

c. 情：合乎實情 the truth

20. 君子強梁以德，小人強梁以力。

——漢・揚雄《太玄・強》

An honourable man's strength lies in his moral
integrity and a mean person demonstrates his force
with his arms.

*—Yang Xiong (53 BC – 18 AD), writer and
philosopher of the Western Han Dynasty*

Terms:

強梁：強有力 strength; force

21. 居視其所親，富視其所與，達視其所舉，
窮視其所不為，貧視其所不取。 ——《史記・魏世家》

See what kind of people one keeps close to under
normal circumstances; see what kind of people one
assists through charity when he becomes wealthy; see
what kind of people one recommends when he is in
power; see what kind of things one refuses to do when
he is in adversity; and see what kind of things one
refuses to take when he is in poverty.

*—Historical Records by Sima Qian
(c.145 or 135 – ? BC) of the Han Dynasty*

Terms:

a. 居：平時 under normal circumstance

b. 與：給與 to give

c. 舉：推舉；推薦 to recommend

22. 君子有過則謝以質，小人有過則謝以文。

——《史記‧孔子世家》

When an honourable man makes a mistake, he
apologizes in all sincerity; when a mean person makes
a mistake, he apologizes by glossing it over.

—*Historical Records by Sima Qian (c.145*
or 135 – ? BC) of the Han Dynasty

Terms:

a. 謝：道歉 to apologize
b. 質：誠實的態度 a sincere attitude
c. 文：掩飾的做法 to cover up; to gloss over

23. 上士忘名，中士立名，下士竊名。

—— 北齊‧顏之推《顏氏家訓‧名實》

An honourable *shi* is indifferent to prestige, an
ordinary *shi* works to establish prestige but an ignoble
shi steals prestige.

—*Admonitions of the Yan's Family by Yan Zhitui*
(531– 590) of the Northern Qi Dynasty

Terms:

a. 上士：品德高尚的士 an honourable *shi*
b. 中士：中等的士，普通的士 an ordinary *shi*; a common *shi*
c. 下士：品德低下的士 an ignoble *shi*

24. 眾君子中不無小人，而群小人內絕無君子。

—— 明‧李夢陽《空同集‧治道篇》

It is likely to find a mean person among virtuous
people, but there can never be a virtuous person
among mean people.

—*Li Mengyang (1473 – 1530), writer of the Ming Dynasty*

Terms:

a. 不無：不一定沒有 not necessarily
b. 絕無：絕對沒有 absolutely not
c. 君子：virtuous people = honourable people

25. 君子有遠慮，小人從邇。 ——《左傳・襄公二十八年》

An honourable man is far-sighted, while a mean person is short-sighted.

—Zuo Zhuan, first chronological history covering the period from 722 BC to 464 BC, attributed to Zuo Qiuming

Terms:

a. 邇（ěr）：近 near
b. 從邇：目光短淺 short-sighted

26. 相馬以輿，相士以居。 ——《孔子家語・子路初見》

1) To judge a horse, put it to the carriage; to judge a scholar, see how he behaves in everyday life.
2) To judge a horse, you need to see how well it pulls the carriage; to judge a scholar, you need to see how he behaves in everyday life.

—Confucius' Teachings collected from ancient classics

Terms:

a. 相（xiàng）：鑒別；察看 to judge
b. 輿：車子 carriage
c. 居：平時 in everyday life

27. 愛憎好惡，古今不鈞；時移俗易，物同賈異。

——《抱朴子・擢才》

The standard of likes and dislikes of the past is not the same as today; as time passes and custom changes, the same thing has different prices.

—*Baopuzi by Ge Hong (284 – 364) of the East Jin Dynasty*

Terms:
a. 愛憎好惡：喜歡和厭惡的東西 likes and dislikes
b. 鈞：均，相同 the same
c. 移、易：變化 to change
d. 賈：通 "價" price

28. 從命利君為之順，從命病君為之諛；逆命利君為之忠，逆命病君為之亂。   ——漢・劉向《說苑・臣術》

Obey the monarch in his interest is called obeisance, and obey the monarch to his detriment is called flattery; disobey the monarch in his interest is called loyalty, and disobey the monarch to his detriment is called rebellion.

—*Liu Xiang (c.77– 6 BC), Confucian scholar and writer of the Western Han Dynasty*

Terms:
a. 從命：遵從君命 to obey the monarch
b. 病：危害 to the detriment of
c. 為：謂，稱作 to be called
d. 逆命：違背……的旨意 to disobey
e. 亂：作亂 to rebel

29. 凡事之不近人情者，鮮不為大姦慝。

—— 宋 · 蘇洵《辨姦論》

Few of the things done against common sense are not done for a sinister purpose.

—Su Xun (1009 – 1066),
writer of the Northern Song Dynasty

Terms:

a. 鮮（xiǎn）：少 few
b. 慝（tè）：邪惡 sinister

30. 富而賑物，德不為難；貧而儉嗇，行非為過。

—— 北齊 · 劉晝《劉子 · 辯施》

It is not hard for the haves to be kind enough to aid the have-nots; it is not too much for the poor to practice thrift to the point of being stingy.

—Liuzi by Liu Zhou (514 – 565), writer
of the Northern Qi Dynasty

Terms:

a. 賑：救濟；施捨 to aid
b. 物：他人 others
c. 儉嗇：節儉，吝嗇 thrifty and stingy
d. 過：過份 too much

31. 小時了了，大未必佳。

—— 南朝 · 宋 · 劉義慶《世説新語 · 言語》

Cleverness in childhood may not be translated into outstanding intelligence in adulthood.

—New Collection of Anecdotes of Celebrities by Liu Yiqing
of the State of Song of the Southern Dynasties

Terms:

了了（liǎo liǎo）：聰明 clever

Note:

When Kong Rong (153 – 208), writer of the Han Dynasty, was ten years old, he went to Luoyang with his father on a visit to their relative Mr.Li Yuanli. Li asked Kong Rong in what way they were related, and Kong Rong replied, my ancestor Confucius was a student of your ancestor Li Er (Laozi), so there has been a long-standing relationship between our two families. The people around were impressed by his quick wit. When Chen Wei, a moderate official, came and was told about what Kong Rong had said, he said, "Cleverness in childhood may not be translated into outstanding intelligence in adulthood." Kong Rong retorted, "You must have been clever in childhood." Chen Wei was embarrassed.

32. 愚者昧於成事，智者見於未萌。　　——《戰國策‧趙策》

The slow-witted finds himself still in the dark when something has happened, but the quick-witted can sense it before it happens.

—Strategies of the Warring States compiled by Liu Xiang (c.77 – 6 BC) of the Western Han Dynasty

Terms:

a.　昧：糊塗 be confused

b.　未萌：還未發生 before something happens

33. 雲厚者雨必猛，弓勁者箭必遠。　　——《抱朴子‧喻蔽》

Thick clouds forecast a heavy rain; a fully pulled bow shoots far.

—Baopuzi by Ge Hong (284 – 364) of the East Jin Dynasty

Comment: Outstanding people will do outstanding things.

34. 義動君子，利動貪人。　　　　　——《漢書・匈奴傳》

An honourable man is moved by humaneness and righteousness, but a greedy man is tempted by wealth and profit.

*—History of Han, chronicle of the Han Dynasty
between 206 BC and 23 AD by Ban Gu (32 – 92)*

35. 君子周而不比，小人比而不周。　　——《論語・為政》

An honourable person gets along with people on friendly terms, but he is not cliquish; a petty-minded person tends to gang up, but he does not get along with people on friendly terms.

*— The Analects, a Confucian classic recording
the words and deeds of Confucius and
his dialogues with his disciples*

Terms:
a. 周：廣泛團結 to be friends with; to get along with people on friendly terms
b. 比：勾結 to gang up with; be cliquish

36. 君子遊道，樂以忘憂；小人全軀，説以忘罪。

——《漢書・楊惲傳》

When an honourable person succeeds in campaigning for his beliefs, he is so delighted that he forgets about his worries; when a petty-minded person manages to keep himself physically intact, he is so pleased that he forgets that he is sinful.

*—History of Han, chronicle of the Han Dynasty
between 206 BC and 23 AD by Ban Gu (32 – 92)*

Terms:

a. 遊道：推行自己的主張 to campaign for one's beliefs
b. 軀：身軀 body
c. 説（yuè）：悦 be pleased

37. 君子和而不同，小人同而不和。　　——《論語・子路》

An honourable person melts differences into harmony without getting along with others blindly; a petty-minded person follows others blindly without trying to settle differences impartially.

—The Analects, a Confucian classic recording the words and deeds of Confucius and his dialogues with his disciples

Terms:

a. 和：和諧 harmony
b. 同：苟同 to get along with others blindly

38. 仁者必有勇，勇者不必有仁。　　——《論語・憲問》

A virtuous man must be courageous but a courageous man may not be virtuous.

—The Analects, a Confucian classic recording the words and deeds of Confucius and his dialogues with his disciples

39. 智而用私，不若愚而用公。　　——《呂氏春秋・貴公》

A quick-witted man with his mind bent on private welfare does not compare with a slow-witted man who is devoted to public welfare.

—Lü's Spring and Autumn Annuals, compiled under the sponsorship of Lü Buwei, Prime Minister of the State of Qin during the late Warring States Period

Terms:
a. 用私：謀私 for private welfare
b. 用公：為公 for the public
c. 不若：不如 not comparable with

40. 君子樂得其道，小人樂得其欲。　　——《史記·樂書》

An honourable man derives pleasure from securing humaneness and righteousness, while a petty-minded person derives pleasure from satisfying his selfish desires.

—Historical Records by Sima Qian
(c.145 or 135 – ? BC) of the Han Dynasty

Terms:
a. 樂得：以……為快樂 to derive pleasure from
b. 道：這裏指"仁義" humaneness and righteousness
c. 欲：私慾 selfish desires

（二）育人舉賢
Educate the People and Recommend the Virtuous

1. 內不可以阿子弟，外不可以隱遠人。
　　——《荀子·君道》

Domestically, one should not be partial to his relatives; externally, one should not ignore the alienated.

—Xunzi by Xun Kuang (313 – 238 BC),
thinker and educator of the Warring States Period

Terms:
a. 阿：偏袒 to be partial to
b. 隱：埋沒 to ignore; to neglect

2.　萬卷藏書宜子弟，十年種木長風煙。

——宋・黃庭堅《郭明甫作西齋於潁尾請予賦詩》二首其一

The collection of ten thousand books facilitates reading by the young children; the trees planted during the past ten years enhances landscape.

—Huang Tingjian (1045 – 1105), poet of the Northern Song Dynasty

Terms:
a. 宜：便於 to facilitate
b. 風煙：風景；景致 landscape

**3.　一年之計，莫如樹穀；十年之計，莫如樹木；
　　終身之計，莫如樹人。**　　　——《管子・權修》

The best thing to do for a year is to sow grains; the best thing to do for ten years is to plant trees; the best thing to do for a hundred years is to educate people and train talents.

—Book of Master Guan Zhong by Guan Zhong (? – 645 BC),
statesman and prime minister of the State of Qi
of early Spring and Autumn Period

Terms:
a. 計：計劃；打算 plan
b. 樹穀：種糧食 to sow grains
c. 樹木：種樹 to plant trees
d. 樹人：培養人 to educate people and train talents

4.　進賢為賢，排賢為不肖。　　——北齊・劉晝《劉子・薦賢》

He who recommends virtuous people is virtuous himself, but he who rejects virtuous people is not virtuous himself.

—Liuzi by Liu Zhou (514 – 565),
writer of the Northern Qi Dynasty

Terms:
a. 進賢：推舉賢人 to recommend virtuous people
b. 不肖：不賢的人 not virtuous

5.　功無大乎進賢。　　　　　　　　——《呂氏春秋・贊能》

1) No service is greater than recommend virtuous people.
2) The greatest service is to recommend virtuous people.

*—Lü's Spring and Autumn Annuals, compiled under the
sponsorship of Lü Buwei, Prime Minister of the State
of Qin during the late Warring States Period*

6.　人必有才也而後能憐才，知音也而後能識曲。

——　清・袁枚《隨園書牘》

He who cherishes talent must be a talent himself;
he who can appreciate music must be well-versed in
temperament.

—Yuan Mei (1716 – 1798), poet of the Qing Dynasty

Terms:
a. 憐才：愛才 to love talent
b. 知音：懂音律 to be well-versed in temperament

7.　知者莫大於知賢，政者莫大於官賢。

——《大戴禮記・主言》

1) The most important thing for a wise man to do is
to discover and understand virtuous and talented
people; the most important thing for a government
administrator to do is to appoint virtuous and
talented people.
2) For a wise man, nothing is more important than

discover and understand virtuous and talented people; for a government administrator, nothing is more important than appoint virtuous and talented people.

—Da Dai's Book of Rites compiled by Dai De,
scholar on rites of the Western Han Dynasty

Terms:

a. 知者：聰明人 wise people
b. 政者：為政者 people who administer government
c. 官賢：使……為官 to appoint somebody to an official position

8. **賢能不待次而舉，不肖不待須而廢。**

——《韓詩外傳》卷五

Virtuous and talented people must be recommended or promoted without delay, wicked people must be removed from office without delay.

—Collection of Comments on Ancient Affairs with Quotes from
The Book of Songs by Han Ying of the Western Han Dynasty

Terms:

a. 次：耽擱 delay
b. 須：耽擱 delay

9. **良弓難張，然可以及高入深；良馬難乘，**
   然可以任重致遠。   ——《墨子‧親士》

A good bow is hard to bend, but the arrow can shoot high and get deep into the target. A good horse is hard to handle, but he can take a heavy load and travel far.

—Mozi, complete works of the Mohist school of
thought founded by Mo Di (c.468 – 376 BC)

Terms:

a. 張：拉 to bend a bow

b. 然：但 but

c. 及：到達 to reach

10. 蓋世必有非常之人，然後有非常之事；
有非常之事，然後有非常之功。

——《漢書‧司馬相如傳下》

1) There must be extraordinary people in the world
   first, then there are extraordinary undertakings and,
   when extraordinary undertakings happen, there are
   extraordinary achievements.

2) There must be extraordinary people in the world
   before there are extraordinary undertakings, and
   extraordinary undertakings before extraordinary
   achievements.

—History of Han, chronicle of the Han Dynasty
between 206 BC and 23 AD by Ban Gu (32 – 92)

Terms:

a. 蓋：句首助詞 a function word, usually placed at the beginning of a
   sentence

b. 非常：不尋常的 extraordinary

11. 以天下與人易，為天下得人難。　——《孟子‧滕文公上》

It is easy to leave the country in somebody's hand,
but it is difficult to find a good monarch to rule the
country.

—Mencius by Meng Ke (c.372 – 289 BC), philosopher
and Confucian scholar of the Warring States Period

Terms:

a. 以天下與人：把國家交與某人 to leave the country in somebody's
   hand

b. 為天下得人：為國家找一個好的國君 to find a competent
   monarch for the country

12. 馬以一圉人而肥，民以一令而樂。

——清‧顧炎武《郡縣論》

When a horse is well-fed by a good feeder, he becomes chubby and strong; when the people of a county are well-administered by a good magistrate, they live in peace and contentment.

*—Gu Yanwu (1613 – 1682), scholar and thinker
of late Ming and early Qing Dynasty*

Terms:

a. 圉 (yǔ) 人：養馬者 a horse feeder

b. 令：縣令 a county magistrate

13. 十步之間，必有茂草；十室之邑，必有俊士。

——漢‧王符《潛夫論‧實貢》

Within a distance of ten paces, there must be luxuriant grass; within a town of ten households, there must be outstanding people.

*—Social Evils through the Eye of a Hermit by Wang Fu
(c.85 – 162), philosopher of the Eastern Han Dynasty*

Terms:

a. 邑：小城 small town

b. 俊士：傑出人才 outstanding people

14. 用其道，不棄其人。　　——《左傳‧定公九年》

1) Since you adopted his doctrine, you should not reject his person.

2) Since his doctrine is adopted, his person should not be rejected.

*—Zuo Zhuan, first chronological history covering
the period from 722 BC to 464 BC, attributed to Zuo Qiuming*

Terms:

道：主張 doctrine

**15. 得十良馬，不若得一伯樂；得十良劍，
不若得一歐冶。**　　　　　　　——《呂氏春秋‧贊能》

Ten admirable horses are not as valuable as a Bo Le;
ten sharp swords are not as valuable as an Ou Ye.

*—Lü's Spring and Autumn Annuals, compiled under the
sponsorship of Lü Buwei, Prime Minister of the State
of Qin during the late Warring States Period*

Terms:

歐冶：春秋時代善鑄劍者 an expert sword maker during the Spring
and Autumn period

16. 國不務大，而務得民心；佐不務多，而務得賢臣。

——《大戴禮記‧保傳》

A country does not have to be very large in size or
population, but it must know how to win the heart
of the people; a monarch does not have to have many
advisors, but he has to have virtuous and talented
court officials to assist him.

*—Da Dai's Book of Rites compiled by Dai De,
scholar on rites of the Western Han Dynasty*

Terms:

a. 不務：不必 not have to
b. 佐：輔佐的人 advisors

17. 家貧則思良妻；國亂則思良相。

——《史記‧魏世家》

1) When the household is impoverished, it thinks of a virtuous and capable housewife; when the country is in turmoil, it thinks of a virtuous and competent prime minister.

2) A poor household calls for a virtuous and capable housewife; a turbulent country calls for a virtuous and competent prime minister.

—Historical Records by Sima Qian (c.145 or 135 – ? BC) of the Han Dynasty

Terms:

a. 國亂：當國家處於動亂之中 when the country is in turmoil

b. 良相：賢良的宰相 virtuous and competent prime minister

18. 簡能而任之，擇善而從之。 ——唐‧魏徵《諫太宗十思疏》

Select the virtuous and talented to take office, and choose good advice to follow.

— "Memorial to Emperor Taizong" by Wei Zheng (580 – 643), statesman of the Tang Dynasty

Terms:

a. 簡：選拔 to select

b. 從：聽從；照辦 to follow

19. 君子尊賢而容眾，嘉善而矜不能。 ——《論語‧子張》

An honourable man is respectful of the virtuous and tolerant to the ordinary, but he acclaims the benevolent and sympathizes with the less capable.

—The Analects, a Confucian classic recording the words and deeds of Confucius and his dialogues with his disciples

Terms:

a. 容眾：容納 to be tolerant to

b. 矜（jīn）：同情 to sympathize with

20. 一言僨事，一人定國。　　　　——《禮記‧大學》

1) One word can ruin things and one man can save the country.

2) An inappropriate remark can mess things up and a phenomenal man can put the country on the right track.

—The Book of Rites, a Confucian classic

Terms:

僨（fèn）事：把事情弄壞 to ruin things; to mess up things

（三）量才授任
Designate Assignment According to Competence

1. 苟有仁人，何必周親？　　　　——《尸子‧綽子》

If there are virtuous people around, why do you have to rely on your closest kinsfolk?

—Shizi by Shi Jiao (c.390 – 330), thinker
and statesman of the Warring States Period

Terms:

a. 苟：如果 if

b. 周親：至親 the dearest and nearest

2.　弓調而後求勁焉，馬服而後求良焉，士信愨而後求
能焉。　　　　　　　　　　　　——《荀子・哀公》

You must adjust the bow first and then expect the
arrow to project far, you must tame the horse first and
then expect it to run fast, you must make sure first
that the *shi* is trustworthy and honest and then expect
him to be competent.

> —*Xunzi by Xun Kuang (313 – 238 BC), thinker*
> *and educator of the Warring States Period*

Terms:
a.　調：協調 to adjust
b.　服：馴服 to tame
c.　信愨（què）：誠實 trustworthy and honest

3.　朽木不可以為柱。　　　　　　——《漢書・劉輔傳》

Rotten wood cannot be used as supporting pillars.

> —*History of Han, chronicle of the Han Dynasty*
> *between 206 BC and 23 AD by Ban Gu (32 – 92)*

4.　彈鳥，則千金不及丸泥之用；縫緝，則長劍不及數
分之針。　　　　　　　　　　　——《抱朴子・備闕》

To shoot birds with a catapult, a thousand pieces of
gold are not as effective as a clay ball; to sew things
up, a long sword is not as effective as a small needle.

> —*Baopuzi by Ge Hong (284 – 364) of the East Jin Dynasty*

Terms:
a.　彈（tán）鳥：用彈弓打鳥 to shoot birds with a catapult
b.　縫緝：縫紉 to sew things with a needle

5. 有大略者不可責以捷巧，有小智者不可任以大功。

—《淮南子・主術訓》

People with strategic resources should not be expected to have shallow skills, people of mediocre intelligence should not be entrusted with significant services.

—Huainanzi by Prince Huainan Liu An (179 – 122 BC)
and some of his followers of the Western Han Dynasty

Terms:

a. 大略：謀略 strategic resources
b. 捷巧：小技藝 shallow skills
c. 大功：功，通 "工"；大事 things of great significance

6. 狐裘雖敝，不可補以黃狗之皮。

—《史記・田敬仲完世家》

Though the fox's fur is worn out, it should not be patched with a yellow dog's.

—Historical Records by Sima Qian (c.145 or 135 – ? BC)
of the Han Dynasty

Terms:

a. 裘：毛皮 fur
b. 敝（bì）：破 to be worn out; to be broken
c. 補以黃狗之皮：用黃狗的皮來補之 to patch with yellow dog's fur

Note:

Originally it means good government officials should not be mixed with corrupt ones. It can also mean good things should not be mixed up with tainted ones.

（四）用眾成事
Make Concerted Efforts

1. 百藥並生，各有所愈。……舟輿異路，俱致行旅。

——漢・牟融《牟子》

All medical herbs grow during the same season, but each has an illness to cure ... Boats and carriages travel in different ways, but both can take their passengers to their destination.

— Mouzi by Mou Rong (170 – ?) of the Han Dynasty

Terms:

a. 舟輿：車船 boats and carriages
b. 行旅：行路之人 travellers

2. 為善與眾行之，為巧與眾能之，此善之善者，巧之巧者也。

——《尹文子・大道上》

When you do good things, do them together with others; when you have deft skills, share them with others. This is the good of good, the deft of deft.

— YinWenzi by Yin Wen of the Warring States Period

Terms:

a. 為善：做好事 to do good things
b. 為巧：掌握巧妙的技術 to have deft skills

3. 雖有至知，萬人謀之。

——《莊子・外物》

Although you are extremely intelligent, you still need to take united wisdom to work things out.

— Zhuangzi by Zhuang Zhou (c.369 – 286 BC)
and his followers of the Warring States Period

Terms:

至知：絕頂聰明 extremely intelligent

4. 林莽之材，猶無可棄者，而況人乎？

——《淮南子‧主術訓》

Even stems of wood from shrubberies should not be discarded, less should the people.

—Huainanzi by Prince Huainan Liu An (179 – 122 BC) and some of his followers of the Western Han Dynasty

Terms:

林莽：灌木叢 shrubberies

5. 物有所宜，不廢其材。   ——漢‧王符《潛夫論‧實貢》

Everything has its usefulness, so useful things should not be discarded.

—Social Evils through the Eye of a Hermit by Wang Fu (c.85 – 162), philosopher of the Eastern Han Dynasty

Terms:

宜：用處 usefulness

6. 雖有絲麻，無棄菅蒯；雖有姬薑，無棄蕉萃。

——《左傳‧成公九年》

Though you have silk and hemp, you mustn't discard wild grass like *jian* and *kuai*, though you have beautiful women like ancient *Ji* and *Jiang*, you mustn't abandon ugly and humble women.

—Zuo Zhuan, first chronological history covering the period from 722 BC to 464 BC, attributed to Zuo Qiuming

Terms:

a. 絲麻：silk and hemp
b. 菅蒯 (jiān kuǎi)：野草 wild grass
c. 姬薑：指古代大國之女人，泛指美女 referring to beautiful women in ancient China
d. 蕉萃：通 "憔悴"，指醜陋低賤的女人 referring to ugly and humble women

7. 積力之所舉，則無不勝也；眾智之所為，
   則無不成也。 ──《淮南子 • 主術訓》

Concerted efforts can raise any object; united wisdom can solve any problem.

*—Huainanzi by Prince Huainan Liu An (179 – 122 BC)
and some of his followers of the Western Han Dynasty*

Terms:

a. 積力：眾人之力 concerted efforts
b. 眾智：眾人的智慧 united wisdom

8. 大匠無棄材，船車用不均；
   錐刀各異能，何所獨卻前？
   ── 三國 • 魏 • 曹植《當欲遊南山行》

A veteran carpenter does not throw away any wood,
Boats and carriages take passengers in different ways;
Awls and knives are used for different purposes,
There is no sense in rating them as superior or inferior.

*—Cao Zhi (192 – 232), poet of the State of Wei
of the Three Kingdoms*

Terms:

a. 大匠：高明的木匠 a veteran carpenter
b. 不均：不同 not the same
c. 卻前：高低之分 superior or inferior

9. 善用人者，若蚈之足，眾而不相害；若脣之與齒，
堅柔相摩而不相敗。　　　　　——《淮南子·說林訓》

He who knows how to make his people work in
harmony is like a crawler which moves its crowded
feet without interfering each other; he who knows
how to make his people work in harmony is like lips
to teeth which do not hurt each other, though the soft
keeps rubbing against the hard.

—Huainanzi by Prince Huainan Liu An (179 – 122 BC)
and some of his followers of the Western Han Dynasty

Terms:

蚈 (qiān)：百足之蟲 a many-footed crawler

10. 百柱載梁，千歲不僵。　　　　——漢·焦贛《焦氏易林》

With one hundred pillars bearing the beam, the beam
will not collapse in one thousand years.

—Jiao Gong of the Han Dynasty

Terms:

僵：這裏指倒塌 to fall; to collapse

11. 金雖克木，而錐鑽不可以伐鄧林；
水雖勝火，而升合不足以救焚山。
　　　　　　　　　　　　　　　——《抱朴子·嘉遁》

Although metal can overcome wood, forests cannot
be felled with awls or drills; although water can
overcome fire, mountain fires cannot be put out with
a *sheng* or *ge* of water.

—Baopuzi by Ge Hong (284 – 364) of the East Jin Dynasty

Terms:

a. 鄧林：此處泛指樹林 forests
b. 升合（gě）：古代較小的容量單位 *sheng* and *ge*, small units of capacity in ancient China

（五）不求全責備
No One is Perfect

1.　人非堯舜，誰能盡善！　　　──唐・李白《與韓荊州書》

As there is no one like Yao or Shun, no one should be expected to be perfect.

—Li Bai (701 – 762), poet of the Tang Dynasty

Terms:

a. 堯舜：古代傳說中的兩個君主 two legendary monarchs; ancient sages
b. 盡善：完美無缺 perfect

2.　能言莫不褒堯，而堯政不必皆得也；
舉世莫不貶桀，而桀事不盡失也。

──《抱朴子・博喻》

Of all those capable of speech, no one failed to praise the ancient sage Yao, but that doesn't mean all of his policies were correct; of all the people in the country, no one failed to condemn Jie, but that doesn't mean everything Jie did was wrong.

—Baopuzi by Ge Hong (284 – 364) of the East Jin Dynasty

Terms:

a. 得：做得正確 correct
b. 桀：中國古代夏朝最後君主，歷史上被認為是暴君 the last ruler of the Xia Dynasty (c.2070 – 1600BC), believed to be a tyrant

c. 失：錯失 wrong

3. 一能之士，各貢所長，出處默語，勿強相兼。

—— 漢・王符《潛夫論・實貢》

Let each person give full play to what he is good at: either take office or withdraw from society, either keep quiet or advocate his views, but he should not be obliged to perform all trades.

—*Social Evils through the Eye of a Hermit by Wang Fu (c.85 – 162), philosopher of the Eastern Han Dynasty*

Terms:

a. 貢：施展 to give full play to
b. 出：出仕；做官 to go out and take an official position
c. 處（chǔ）：隱居 to withdraw from society
d. 默：不宣傳自己的主張或評論時政 to keep quiet about one's views or current affairs
e. 語：宣傳自己的主張或評論時政 to advocate one's views or criticize current affairs

4. 論大功者不錄小過，舉大美者不疵細瑕。

——《漢書・陳湯傳》

In evaluating one's meritorious services, his insignificant faults should not be taken into account; in citing one's honourable virtue, his minor flaws can be neglected.

—*History of Han, chronicle of the Han Dynasty between 206 BC and 23 AD by Ban Gu (32 – 92)*

Terms:

a. 不錄：不記；不計較 not to take into account
b. 疵（cī）：把……當作毛病 to regard something as a flaw
c. 瑕（xiá）：玉上的斑點，小毛病 spots on jade, here it means minor faults

5. 明者舉大略細，不忮不求。   ——《抱朴子‧接疏》

Sensible people focus their attention on important things and ignore trivialities, and they are not jealous or overcritical of others.

—Baopuzi by Ge Hong (284 – 364) of the East Jin Dynasty

Terms:

a. 忮（zhì）：嫉恨 jealous
b. 求：苛求 overcritical

6. 君子不責備於一人。   ——《淮南子‧泛論訓》

An honourable man does not demand anyone to be flawless.

—Huainanzi by Prince Huainan Liu An (179 – 122 BC) and some of his followers of the Western Han Dynasty

Terms:

a. 責：要求 to demand
b. 備：完美 perfect

7. 凡有角者無上齒，果實繁者木必庳。

——《呂氏春秋‧博志》

Horned animals have no sharp teeth; trees laden with fruit must be low.

—Lü's Spring and Autumn Annuals, compiled under the sponsorship of Lü Buwei, Prime Minister of the State of Qin during the late Warring States Period

Terms:

a. 上齒：利齒 sharp teeth
b. 庳（bì）：低矮 low

8. 任人之長不強其短，任人之工不強其拙。

——《晏子春秋‧內篇‧問上》

Give full play to one's strength and do not demand too much of him where he is weak; give full play to one's deft skills and do not demand too much of him where he is clumsy.

— Yanzi's Spring and Autumn Annals, supposedly written by Yan Ying (? – 500 BC), minister of the State of Qi during the Spring and Autumn Period

Terms:

a. 強（qiǎng）：強求 to demand too much

b. 工：巧 deft skills

9. 不知無害於君子，知之無損於小人。

——《尹文子‧大道上》

When an honourable man is ignorant of anything, it doesn't injure his noble character; when a mean person is well informed of something, it doesn't rule him out as a mean person.

— YinWenzi by Yin Wen of the Warring States Period

10. 人雖賢，不能左畫方，右畫圓。　——《史記‧龜策列傳》

Though one may be a capable man, he cannot draw a square with his left hand and, simultaneously, a circle with his right hand.

— Historical Records by Sima Qian (c.145 or 135 – ? BC) of the Han Dynasty

11. 天地無全功，聖人無全能，萬物無全用。

——《列子·天瑞篇》

Neither Heaven nor Earth has all round functions, no sage has all-round capabilities, and nothing in the world has all round usefulness.

—Liezi, Taoist classical work by Lie Yukou of the Warring States Period

Comment: Everyone and everything in the world has his and its limitations.

12. 仲尼見人一善，而忘其百非；鮑叔聞人一過，而終身不忘。

—— 北齊·劉晝《劉子·妄瑕》

When Confucius finds someone has some merit, he forgets all of his demerits; when Bao Shu hears someone has committed a fault, he will not forget it all his life.

—Liuzi by Liu Zhou (514 – 565), writer of the Northern Qi Dynasty

Terms:
a. 仲尼：孔子 Confucius
b. 鮑叔：鮑叔牙 an official of the State of Qi during the Spring and Autumn Period

Comment: Confucius' and Bao Shu's attitudes towards people are different: one is generous and tolerant, the other narrow-minded.

（六）不以尊卑長幼論人
One Should Not Be Judged by Age and Status

1. 美玉生磐石，寶劍出龍淵。　　——三國・魏・曹植《雜詩》

Beautiful jade is derived from big rocks; precious swords are tempered with the water from Dragon Spring.

—Cao Zhi (192 – 232), poet of the State of Wei of the Three Kingdoms

Terms:

a. 磐（pán）石：大石頭 big rocks
b. 生：出自 to be derived from
c. 龍淵：龍泉之水 water from the Dragon Spring

Comment: Beautiful things are found in commonplace things. Honourable people come from the humble.

2. 才苟適治，不問世胄；智苟能謀，奚妨秕行。

——北齊・劉晝《劉子・薦賢》

If one has the talent to run state affairs, there is no need to bother about his family background; if one is strategically resourceful, it does not matter if he has some unbecoming behaviour.

—Liuzi by Liu Zhou (514 – 565), writer of the Northern Qi Dynasty

Terms:

a. 苟（gǒu）：如果 if
b. 世胄（zhòu）：世家，指貴族後裔 noble family
c. 奚（xī）妨：何妨 why not; what does it matter
d. 秕（bǐ）行：不良行為 unbecoming behaviour

3. 淤泥解作白蓮藕，糞壤能開黃玉花。

　　　　　　　　　　—— 宋·黃庭堅《次韻中玉水仙花》二首之一

White lotus root grows out of mud and yellow
narcissus springs up from dung and dirt.

—*Huang Tingjian (1045 – 1105),*
poet of the Northern Song Dynasty

Comment: Moral integrity and capabilities are more important
than family background.

4. 既有其類，便有出乎其類者。　—— 清·袁枚《隨園書牘》

1) Since there are different social strata, there must be
   outstanding people in each category.
2) Since people are categorized, there must be
   outstanding ones in each category.

—*Yuan Mei (1716 – 1798), poet of the Qing Dynasty*

5. 是非之處，不可以貴賤尊卑論也。　——《文子·上仁》

1) The judgment of right or wrong should be
   independent of social status.
2) The judgment of right or wrong must not be
   interfered by social status.

—*Wenzi, a Taoist work by unknown author*
of the Warring States Period

Comment: There is a standard by which to judge what is right
and what is wrong. It has nothing to do with social status. The
things people of high status say or do may not be right; the
things people of low status say or do may not be wrong.

6. 相馬失之瘦，相士失之貧。　　　──《史記・滑稽列傳》

A horse may fail to be chosen because it is scrawny; a *shi* may fail to get appointed because he comes from a poor family.

　　　　　　　　　　　—Historical Records by Sima Qian
(c.145 or 135 – ? BC) of the Han Dynasty

7. 官無常貴，民無終賤。　　　──《墨子・尚賢上》

State officials cannot sit on their high positions forever, and the common people cannot remain humble all their lives.

　　　　　　　　　　　—Mozi, complete works of the Mohist school of
thought founded by Mo Di (c.468 – 376 BC)

8. 從來天下士，只在布衣中。　　　──清・屈大均《魯連台》

The most virtuous and talented *shi* of the country are ever to be found among the common people.

　　　　　　　　　　　—Qu Dajun (1630 – 1696), writer of early Qing Dynasty

Terms:
a.　天下士：德才出眾之士 the virtuous and talented *shi*
b.　布衣：平民百姓 the common people

9. 弟子不必不如師，師不必賢於弟子。

　　　　　　　　　　　──唐・韓愈《師說》

The student is not necessarily inferior to his teacher, and the teacher is not necessarily superior to his student.

　　　　　　　　　　　—Han Yu (768 – 824), writer and philosopher
of the Tang Dynasty

10. 宣父猶能畏後生，丈夫未可輕年少。

——唐・李白《上李邕》

Even Confucius holds the young people in high esteem, so the aged should not look down upon the young.

—Li Bai (701 – 762), poet of the Tang Dynasty

Terms:
a. 宣父：孔子 Confucius
b. 後生：年輕人 the young people
c. 畏：敬重 respect
d. 丈夫：老者；長者 the aged, referring to Li Yi, who was 23 years older than Li Bai

11. 後來者居上。

——《史記・汲鄭列傳》

1) One can come ahead from behind.
2) The one who has lagged behind can come ahead of others sooner or later.

—Historical Records by Sima Qian
(c.145 or 135 – ? BC) of the Han Dynasty

（七）不以貌取人
Looks Can Be Deceptive

1. 志遠學不逮，名高實難副。

——梁啟超錄楊度詩句

Soaring ambitions are hard to fulfill with limited learning, and a high-sounding name is hard to match realities.

—quoted from Yang Du, statesman of late Qing Dynasty,
by the modern scholar Liang Qichao (1873 – 1929)

Terms:
a. 逮（dài）：及；達到 to fulfill; to reach

b. 副：相稱 to match

2. 落落之玉，或亂乎石；碌碌之石，時似乎玉。

—— 南朝 · 梁 · 劉勰《文心雕龍 · 總術》

Hard jade is sometimes mistaken for rock; and beautiful rock sometimes looks like jade.

—The Literary Mind and the Carving of the Dragon
by Liu Xie (c.465 – 532) of the State of Liang of the Southern Dynasties

Terms:
a. 落落：形容石頭堅硬 an adjective modifying the hardness of rock
b. 碌碌（lù）：形容玉美好 an adjective describing the beauty of jade

3. 人有盜而富者，富者未必盜；有廉而貧者，
貧者未必廉。   ——《淮南子 · 說林訓》

There are people who become rich by theft, but not all rich people are thieves; there are people who become poor because they are incorrupt, but not all poor people are incorruptible.

—Huainanzi by Prince Huainan Liu An (179 – 122 BC)
and some of his followers of the Western Han Dynasty

4. 狗不以善吠為良，人不以善言為賢。

——《莊子 · 徐無鬼》

1) Dogs good in barking should not be regarded as good dogs; eloquent people should not be regarded as virtuous and talented.

2) Dogs good in barking are not necessarily good dogs; eloquent people are not necessarily virtuous and talented.

—Zhuangzi by Zhuang Zhou (c.369 – 286 BC)
and his followers of the Warring States Period

5. 官達者未必當其位，譽美者未必副其名。

　　　　　　　　　　　　　　　——《抱朴子‧博喻》

High-ranking officials may not be qualified for their positions and prestigious people may not deserve the prestige they enjoy (or be equal to what they really are).

—Baopuzi by Ge Hong (284 – 364) of the East Jin Dynasty

Terms:
a. 達：官職高 high-ranking position
b. 當：稱職 to be qualified for

6. 善人者，不善人之師；不善人者，善人之資。

　　　　　　　　　　　　　　——《老子‧道經二十七》

A moral person is the teacher of an immoral one and an immoral person can provide a warning against immorality.

—Laozi by Li Er (李耳), philosopher of late Spring
and Autumn Period, and founder of Taoism

Terms:
資：借鑒 in this case it means learning a lesson from somebody

（八）人老智可用
The Aged Has More with Wisdom

1. 色，老而衰；智，老而多。　　　——《戰國策‧趙策》

Good looks withers with age, but wisdom grows with age.

—Strategies of the Warring States compiled by Liu Xiang
(c.77 – 6 BC) of the Western Han Dynasty

Terms:
色：美麗的容貌 good looks

2. 古來存老馬，不必取長途。　　　──唐・杜甫《江漢》

Since ancient times people believe that old horses
know their way better, so there is no need to make
them travel long distances.

—Du Fu (712 – 770), poet of the Tang Dynasty

Terms:
老馬：意即老馬識途 old horses know the way better

（九）用人信人
Trust the Person Employed

1. 疑則勿用，用則勿疏。疑則勿用，用則勿疏。

　　　　　── 唐・白居易《策林三・君不行臣事》

If you mistrust a person, do not employ him; but once
you decide to employ him, do not distance him.

—Bai Juyi (772 – 846), poet of the Tang Dynasty

2. 恩厚無不使。　　　──《史記・魯仲連鄒陽列傳》

Generous kindness is repaid with willing service.

—Historical Records by Sima Qian (c.145
or 135 – ? BC) of the Han Dynasty

（十）才能品德特別出眾者
Outstanding People

1.　仰之彌高，鑽之彌堅。　　　　——《論語·子罕》

The more I look up to him, the higher he towers; the more I study him, the more profound he becomes.

—The Analects, a Confucian classic recording
the words and deeds of Confucius and his dialogues with his disciples

Terms:

a. 彌（mí）：更加；愈加 the more
b. 堅：深奧 profound

Note:

This is what Confucius' favourite disciple Yan Hui said about his Master.

2.　聞而知之，聖也；見而知之，智也。　——《文子·道德》

He who gets real knowledge through the ear is a sage; he who gets real knowledge through the eye is intelligent.

—Wenzi, a Taoist work by unknown
author of the Warring States Period

3.　注焉而不滿，酌焉而不竭。　　　——《莊子·齊物論》

Fill it, and it never overflows; empty it, and it never gets dried up.

—Zhuangzi by Zhuang Zhou (c.369 – 286 BC)
and his followers of the Warring States Period

Terms:

a. 注：往容器裏灌液體 to pour liquid into a container
b. 酌：往外倒液體 to empty liquid from a container
c. 竭：盡 to dry up

4.　春蘭秋菊，各一時之秀也！　　——唐・顏師古《隋遺錄》

Spring orchid and autumnal chrysanthemum are each the precious plant of its season.

—Yan Shigu (581 – 645), exegete of
ancient texts of the Tang Dynasty

（十一）成才須磨練
Talent is Cultivated through Hardships

1.　必恃自直之箭，百世無矢；恃自圓之木，
　　千世無輪矣。　　　　　——《韓非子・顯學》

1) If arrows have to be made from naturally straight bamboo, there will be no arrows in the next one hundred years; if carriage wheels have to be made from naturally round logs, there will be no wheels in the next one thousand years.

2) If one has to rely on naturally straight bamboo for arrows, there will be no arrows in the next one hundred years; if one has to rely on naturally round logs for carriage wheels, there will be no wheels in the next one thousand years.

—Hanfeizi by Han Fei (c.280 – 233 BC), legalist
and statesman of the late Warring States Period

Terms:

a. 恃（shì）：依靠 to rely on

b. 自直：天生直 naturally straight

c. 箭：箭竹，一種竹子 a type of bamboo

d. 矢：箭（桿）arrow

e. 自圓：天生圓 naturally round

f. 輪：車輪 carriage wheels

2. 居不隱者，思不遠也；身不危者，志不廣也。

——《劉子·激通》

If one has not had low and humble experiences, he
cannot think far into the future; if one has not endured
adversities, he cannot cherish great ambitions.

—Liuzi by Liu Zhou (514 – 565), writer
of the Northern Qi Dynasty

Terms:

a. 居：處境 situation
b. 隱：卑微 low and humble
c. 思：考慮 to think

3. 天將降大任於斯人也，必先苦其心志，
勞其筋骨，餓其體膚，空乏其身，
行拂亂其所為。

——《孟子·告子下》

When Heaven is going to entrust this man with a great
mission, He will first of all make his mind suffer,
tire his body, subject him to hunger and poverty, and
confound him in his undertakings.

—Mencius by Meng Ke (c.372 – 289 BC), philosopher
and Confucian scholar of the Warring States Period

Terms:

a. 苦：使苦惱 to make somebody suffer mentally
b. 勞：使勞累 to tire
c. 空乏：使窮困 to subject ...to poverty
d. 拂亂：擾亂 to confound; to confuse

4. 英雄不失路，何以成功名？　　——清・屈大均《贈朱士稚》

Heroes without suffering setbacks cannot succeed in
attaining scholarly degrees or official positions.

—Qu Dajun (1630 – 1696), writer of early Qing Dynasty

Terms:

a. 失路：找不到出路，也指失意，受挫折 It means literally one
cannot find his way out; in this context, it means to suffer setbacks or
frustrations.

b. 功名：封建時代指科舉稱號或官職名位 In feudal times, it referred
to scholarly degrees conferred on or official appointments assigned to
scholars after passing imperial civil examinations.

5. 莫道讒言如浪深，莫言遷客似沙沈。
千淘萬漉雖辛苦，吹盡寒沙始到金。

——唐・劉禹錫《浪淘沙》九首之八

Don't say malicious slanders are like dark waves,
Don't say the relegated is like sinking sand. It is hard
indeed to be washed by the waves, But, with the sand
washed off, the gold appears.

—Liu Yuxi (772 – 842), writer and philosopher of the Tang Dynasty

四、處境
Situations Make the Difference

1. 心有千載憂，身無一日閒。 　　——唐·白居易《秋山》

My heart is filled with concerns about the next one thousand years, and my body enjoys no leisure for a single day.

—Bai Juyi (772 – 846), poet of the Tang Dynasty

2. 慶雲未時興，雲龍潛作魚。 　——三國·魏·曹植《言志》

When auspicious clouds have not appeared in the sky, the cloud dragon will remain in water in the form of a fish.

—Cao Zhi (192 – 232), poet of the
State of Wei of the Three Kingdoms

Terms:
a. 慶雲：祥雲 auspicious clouds
b. 雲龍：《易經》有 "雲從龍" 之説 *The Book of Changes* says when there are clouds in the sky, the dragon will come out of water and soar up into the sky on clouds.

3. 大道如青天，我獨不得出。

　　　　　　——唐·李白《行路難》三首之二

Life opens up a road as wide as the sky, but there is no way out for me alone.

—Li Bai (701 – 762), poet of the Tang Dynasty

4. 鯨魚失水，則制於螻蟻。   ——《文子‧上仁》

When the whale is out of water, it leaves itself at the mercy of mole crickets and ants.

—Wenzi, a Taoist work by unknown author of the Warring States Period

Terms:

a. 失水：離開水 be out of water
b. 制於：受制於 be at the mercy of; under control of; to be harassed by
c. 螻蟻：螻蛄和螞蟻 mole crickets and ants

5. 猛虎在深山，百獸震恐，及在阱檻之中，
搖尾而求食。   —— 漢‧司馬遷《報任安書》

When a tiger roams around in the mountain, all other animals get panic stricken; when it is trapped or caged, it wags its tail for food.

— "Letter to Ren An" by Sima Qian (c.145 or 135 – ? BC) of the Han Dynasty

6. 書當快意讀易盡，客有可人期不來。
世事相違每如此，好懷百歲幾回開！
          —— 宋‧陳師道《絕句》

An interesting read is easy to finish,
An agreeable guest is hard to expect.
Worldly affairs often defy your wishes like this,
How many times can life kindle
    paroxysms of joy in me!

—Chen Shidao (1053 – 1102), poet of the Northern Song Dynasty

Terms:

a. （書當）快意：讀來使人愉快的（書）(books) you enjoy reading
b. 讀易盡：容易讀完 easy to finish

c. 可人：合人意 agreeable; pleasant to be with
d. 期：期待 to expect
e. 好懷：好心情；心情舒暢 heart filled with joy

7.　屋漏更遭連夜雨。　　　　　　　　——明‧高則誠《琵琶記》

The leaky room is being plagued by continued rains.

—Gao Zecheng, playwright of the Ming Dynasty

8.　既不能令，又不受命，是絕物也。　——《孟子‧離婁上》

1) There is no hope for one who cannot issue orders, nor can he take orders.
2) One is hopeless if he cannot issue orders on the one hand, or obey orders on the other.

—Mencius by Meng Ke (c.372 – 289 BC), philosopher and Confucian scholar of the Warring States Period

Terms:
a. 令：命令 to order
b. 命：命令 orders
c. 絕物：無用之人 a hopeless person

9.　獸窮則齧，鳥窮則啄，人窮則詐。　——《韓詩外傳》卷二

Animals forced in a dead end will bite, birds forced in a dead end will strike with the beak, and men forced in a dead end will deceive.

—Collection of Comments on Ancient Affairs with Quotes from The Book of Songs by Han Ying of the Western Han Dynasty

五、 世態人情
Ways of the World

（一）貧富懸殊
The Poor and the Rich

1. 一叢深色花，十戶中人賦。

——唐・白居易《秦中吟・買花》

A bunch of red peonies is worth the taxes paid by ten average peasant households.

—Bai Juyi (772 – 846), poet of the Tang Dynasty

Terms:
a. 一叢：一束 a bunch of
b. 中人：中等人家 moderate / average household
c. 賦：賦稅 tax

Comment: Vast is the division between the rich and the poor!

2. 採得百花成蜜後，為誰辛苦為誰甜？

——唐・羅隱《蜂》

Having sucked one hundred flowers and fermented the honey, who has it laboured for and who is to taste the sweet honey, I wonder.

—Luo Yin (833 – 909), writer and poet of the Tang Dynasty

3. 用貧求富，農不如工，工不如商，
   刺繡文不如倚市門。 ——《史記·貨殖列傳》

From rags to riches, farming does not benefit as much
as handicraft, handicraft not as much as business and,
for women, embroidery does not benefit as much as
walking the streets.

*—Historical Records by Sima Qian (c.145
or 135 – ? BC) of the Han Dynasty*

Terms:
a. 刺繡文：指婦女繡花 (referring to women) to embroider
b. 倚市門：指在公共場合賣俏為娼 (referring to women) to walk the
   streets

Note:
Sima Qian took these phenomena as a social tragedy.

4. 朱門酒肉臭，路有凍死骨。
   ——唐·杜甫《自京赴奉先縣詠懷五百字》

Meat and wine are getting rotten behind the red gates;
the bones of those frozen to death are lying on the
road.

—Du Fu (712 – 770), poet of the Tang Dynasty

Terms:
朱門：朱漆大門，喻有錢人家 big gates painted red, a metaphor for
the rich

5. 天之道，損有餘而補不足；
   人之道則不然，損不足以奉有餘。
   ——《老子·德經七十七》

The law of Heaven is to take from the haves and give
it to the have-nots; the law of man is different, taking

from the have-nots and offering it to the haves.

—Laozi by Li Er（李耳）, philosopher of late Spring
and Autumn Period, and founder of Taoism

Terms:
a. 天之道：自然法則 / 規律 the law of Heaven; the law of nature
b. 人之道：人類社會法則 / 規律 the law of man
c. 奉：供奉 to offer to

Comment: The rich becomes richer at the expense of the poor, and the poor becomes poorer being exploited by the rich.

6. 公道世間唯白髮，貴人頭上不曾饒。

—— 唐 · 杜牧《送隱者一絕》

Of all things in the world, only white hair is fair; it grows on the heads of high-ranking officials all the same.

—Du Mu (803 – 852), writer and poet of the Tang Dynasty

Terms:
a. 公道：公平 fair
b. 唯：只有 only
c. 饒：放過 to spare

7. 壽不利貧只利富。   —— 宋 · 呂南公《勿願壽》

1) Longevity is only good for the rich, but not for the poor.
2) Longevity is something only for the rich to enjoy, but not for the poor.

—Lü Nangong (c.1047 – 1086) of the Northern Song Dynasty

8.   貧疑陋巷春偏少，貴想豪家月最明。

——唐・韋莊《與東吳生相遇》

Being a poor man residing in the humble lane, I doubt
if there is much spring around, but I guess the moon
must cast more light to the ostentatious mansions of
those high-ranking officials.

—Wei Zhuang (c.836 – 910), poet of the Tang Dynasty

9.   在貴多忘賤，為恩誰能博？狐白足禦冬，
焉念無衣客？

—— 三國・魏・曹植《贈丁儀》

One enjoying a high position forgets his humble
friends. Who is generous enough to spread bounties?
When one wears a fox fur coat to keep himself warm,
How can he care about those scantily clad?

—Cao Zhi (192 – 232), poet of the State of Wei of the Three Kingdoms

Terms:
a. 在貴：身處尊貴地位 in a high position
b. 賤：卑賤的朋友 humble friends
c. 為恩誰能博：誰能廣施恩德 who cares to spread bounties．
d. 狐白：貴重的狐皮外衣 precious fox fur coat
e. 念：顧及 to care about

10. 大道之行也，天下為公……大道既隱，天下為家。

——《禮記・禮運》

When Confucian doctrine of universal harmony gets
under way, the country becomes public property
…When Confucian doctrine of universal harmony is
not practiced, the country becomes private property.

—The Book of Rites, a Confucian classic

Terms:

a. 大道：即儒家所主張的大同社會的政治 Confucian doctrine of universal harmony

b. 隱：消失 not practiced

c. 為家：屬私家 to become private property

（二）世事滄桑
Vicissitudes of Life

1. 大江東去，浪淘盡千古風流人物。

—— 宋‧蘇軾《念奴嬌‧赤壁懷古》

1) With the Yangtze River flowing eastward, all the great and glorious elements since ancient times have been washed away by its torrential waves.

2) The Yangtze River flows eastward, its torrential waves washing away all the great and glorious elements since ancient times.

—Su Shi (1037 – 1101), alias Su Dongpo,
poet of the Northern Song Dynasty

2. 今人不見古時月，今月曾經照古人。

—— 唐‧李白《把酒問月》

Today's people have not seen the ancient moon, but today's moon has shone on the ancient people.

—Li Bai (701 – 762), poet of the Tang Dynasty

Comment: The moon is eternal, but man is mortal.

3. 庭樹不知人去盡，春來還發舊時花。

—— 唐・岑參《山房春事》二首其二

Unaware that the host and hostess of the house are already gone, the trees in the courtyard blossom all the same when spring comes.

—*Cen Shen (c.714 – 770), poet of the Tang Dynasty*

4. 舊時王謝堂前燕，飛入尋常百姓家。

—— 唐・劉禹錫《烏衣巷》

Swallows that nested in front of the halls of the Wangs and Xies in the past have now flown into the houses of the ordinary folks.

—*Liu Yuxi (772 – 842), poet of the Tang Dynasty*

Terms:

王、謝：東晉兩個貴族，王導和謝安 two prominent aristocrats during the East Jin Dynasty (317 – 420), *Wang Dao* and *Xie An*

5. 南朝四百八十寺，多少樓台煙雨中。

—— 唐・杜牧《江南春》

Of all the 480 temples built during the Southern Dynasties, how many of them are still standing there in the misty rain?

—*Du Mu (803 – 852), poet of the Tang Dynasty*

Comment: Although the landscape is the same, the temples have dilapidated and the monarchs who had built them are all gone.

6. 千古興亡多少事，悠悠，不盡長江滾滾流。

—— 宋·辛棄疾《南鄉子·登京口北固亭有懷》

1) How many rises and falls have there been in the world since ancient times! They are all gone like the waves of the ever-flowing Yangtze River.

2) How many rises and falls have there been in the world since ancient time! They have all become history like the gone waves of the Yangtze River.

—*Xin Qiji (1140 – 1207), poet of the Southern Song Dynasty*

7. 高山為淵，深谷為陵。　　　　　——《抱朴子·黃白》

High mountains can become pools and deep valleys can become hills.

—*Baopuzi by Ge Hong (284 – 364) of the East Jin Dynasty*

六、納言
Accept Good Advice

（一）博聽 Remain Open to Advice

1. 言之者無罪，聞之者足以戒。 ——《毛詩序》

He who speaks out is not guilty; he who hears it should take it as a forewarning.

— "Preface" to Mao Poetry which is believed to have been compiled and passed down by Mao Heng and Mao Chang of early Western Han Dynasty

Comment: Part of the purpose of poetry is to voice a warning, but the poet should not be held guilty.

2. 異於己而不非者，公於求善也。 ——《戰國策·趙策》

If you don't invalidate the arguments of those who are at variance with you, that is the fair attitude toward finding right ways of doing things.

—Strategies of the Warring States compiled by Liu Xiang (c.77 – 6 BC) of the Western Han Dynasty

Terms:
a. 非：否定 to invalidate
b. 公：公正 be fair
c. 善：正確的做法 the right way of doing things

3. 堯有欲諫之鼓，舜有誹謗之木，湯有司過之士，
武王有戒慎之。　　　　　　　　——《呂氏春秋·自知》

Yao provided a drum for his advisors to thump, Shun
set up a wooden column for people at odds with him
to write their views on, Tang appointed officials for
correcting his mistakes, and Emperor Wu of the Zhou
Dynasty had a rattle-drum available for people to warn
him with.

—Lü's Spring and Autumn Annuals, compiled under the
sponsorship of Lü Buwei, Prime Minister of the State
of Qin during the late Warring States Period

Terms:
a. 堯、舜：古代傳說中的兩個君主 legendary sage kings in ancient
times
b. 湯：商朝開國皇帝 founder and the first emperor of the Shang
Dynasty (1600 – 1046BC)
c. 武王：周朝開國皇帝 first emperor of the Zhou Dynasty
(1046 – 256 BC)
d. 鞀 (táo)：古代的一種鼓 an ancient drum

4. 同乎己者未必可用，異於我者未必可忽也。
　　　　　　　　　　　　　　　　——《抱朴子·清鑒》

Those who are of the same views as you may not
qualify for office; those who are at odds with you may
not be the ones to be neglected.

—Baopuzi by Ge Hong (284 – 364) of the East Jin Dynasty

Terms:
忽：不重視 to neglect

（二）不因人取言
Make Judicious Judgments of One's Words

1. 聖人千慮，必有一失；愚人千慮，必有一得。

—— 《晏子春秋・內篇・雜下》

In a sage's careful considerations there must /
might be something ill conceived; in a fool's careful
considerations there must / might be something well
conceived.

*—Yanzi's Spring and Autumn Annals, supposedly written
by Yan Ying (? – 500 BC), minister of the State of Qi
during the Spring and Autumn Period*

Terms:

a. 失：考慮不周 ill-considered
b. 得：考慮得當；考慮合理；考慮周到 well-considered

2. 狂夫之言，聖人擇焉。　　　　——《史記・淮陰侯列傳》

Even in the remarks made by a presumptuous person,
there is something for the sage to choose and follow.

*—Historical Records by Sima Qian (c.145
or 135 – ? BC) of the Han Dynasty*

Terms:

狂夫：狂妄的人 a presumptuous person

3. 愚者陳意，而知者論焉。 ——《戰國策·趙策》

Even in the opinions uttered by a fool, there is
something for the wise man to choose and follow.

—Strategies of the Warring States compiled by Liu Xiang
(c.77 – 6 BC) of the Western Han Dynasty

Terms:
a. 陳意：陳述意見；説話 to utter an opinion
b. 論：通 "掄"，意為選擇 to choose

4. 布穀鳴於孟夏，蟋蟀吟於始秋。

——《後漢書·襄楷列傳》

Cuckoo calls in early summer, and cricket chirps in
early autumn.

—History of Eastern Han by Fan Ye (398 – 445), historian
of the State of Song of the Southern Dynasties

Comment: Even birds and insects are trustworthy creatures. They
never fail to come in the season when they are expected.

（三）以實核言
Respect Reality

1. 經目之事，猶恐未真；背後之言，豈能全信？

——《金瓶梅》

Sometimes you have misgivings about the
truthfulness of what you see with your eyes; how can
you fully believe what you hear with your ears?

—Plum in the Gold Vase, a novel
first published in early 17th century

2.   東村裏雞生鳳，南莊上馬變牛。

——元・無名氏《商調・梧葉兒・嘲謊人》

A hen has given birth to a phoenix in the East Village
and a horse has given birth to a cow in the South
Village.

—An anonymous poet of the Yuan Dynasty

Comment: This is a mock at storytellers.

3.   崇人之德，揚人之美，非道諛也；正言直行，
指人之過，非毀疵也。   ——《韓詩外傳》卷六

Praising one's virtue and making one's merits known
is not flattering; being forthright and frankly pointing
out where one is wrong is not slandering.

*—Collection of Comments on Ancient Affairs with Quotes
from The Book of Songs by Han Ying of the Western Han Dynasty*

Terms:
a. 崇：推崇 to praise
b. 道諛 (yú)：說奉承話 to flatter
c. 毀疵：毀謗 to slander; to malign

4.   樂取於人以為善，聖人也；無稽之言勿聽，
亦聖人也。   —— 清・袁枚《隨園詩話》

He who is ready to learn from the merits of others in
order to do good is a sage; he who refuses to listen to
unfounded talk is a sage, too.

—Yuan Mei (1716 – 1798), poet of the Qing Dynasty

Terms:
a. 樂取：喜歡吸取 ready to learn from; ready to adopt
b. 無稽之言：沒有根據的話 unfounded talk

5. 聽者事之候也，計者事之機也。

——《史記‧淮陰侯列傳》

If one listens to what others have to say, that is the herald of success; if one plans the steps to take, that is the key to success.

—Historical Records by Sima Qian
(c.145 or 135 – ? BC) of the Han Dynasty

Terms:
a. 候：徵兆 sign; herald
b. 機：關鍵 key

6. 兩喜必多溢美之言，兩怒必多溢惡之言。

——《莊子‧人間世》

When two countries are on friendly terms, there are many good words to say about each other; when they are on hostile terms, there are many bad words to say against each other.

—Zhuangzi by Zhuang Zhou (c.369 – 286 BC)
and his followers of the Warring States Period

Terms:
a. 兩喜：兩國交好 two countries on friendly terms
b. 溢：過多的 too many
c. 兩惡：兩國交惡 two countries on hostile terms

7. 得其言，不若得其所以言。　　——《淮南子‧泛論訓》

To understand what one says is not as important as to find out why he says so.

—Huainanzi by Prince Huainan Liu An (179 – 122 BC)
and some of his followers of the Western Han Dynasty

Terms:

a. 不若：不如 not as good as...

b. 所以：⋯⋯的原因 the reason why

8. 聽其言必責其用，觀其行必求其功。

——《韓非子・六反》

When you hear what one says, you must find out about its practical value; when you see what one does, you must find out about its ultimate effect.

—Hanfeizi by Han Fei (c.280 – 233 BC), legalist and statesman of late Warring States Period

Terms:

a. 責：追究 to find out

b. 用：實用價值 practical value

c. 求：探求 to find out

d. 功：效果 effect

（四）聽直排諛

Take Honest Words and Reject Flattering Ones

1. 良玉不雕，美言不文。　　——漢・揚雄《法言・寡見》

1) Beautiful jade does not need cutting and polishing, and well-meant words do not need embellishing.

2) Beautiful jade needn't be cut and polished, and well-meant words needn't be embellished.

—Yang Xiong (53 BC – 18 AD), writer and philosopher of the Western Han Dynasty

Terms:

文：修飾 to embellish; to dress up

2. 君子贈人以軒，不若以言。 ——《晏子春秋・內篇・雜上》

When an honourable man bids farewell to a friend, it's better to give him advice instead of an elegant carriage.

— Yan Zi's Spring and Autumn Annals, supposedly written by Yan Ying (? – 500 BC), minister of the State of Qi during the Spring and Autumn Period

Terms:

a. 軒（xuān）：古代華貴馬車 an elegant carriage used in ancient times

b. 言：臨別贈言 farewell advice

3. 君子重正言之惠，賢於軒璧之贈。

——北齊・劉晝《劉子・貴言》

An honourable man values the benefit of frank and pertinent advice more than the gift of an elegant carriage or precious jade.

— Liuzi by Liu Zhou (514 – 565), writer of the Northern Qi Dynasty

Terms:

a. 重：看重；重視 to value

b. 惠：好處 benefit

c. 賢於：比……好 better than

d. 軒璧：馬車和美玉 carriage and jade

4. 鏡無見疵之罪，道無明過之怨。　　——《韓非子‧觀行》

A looking glass is not to be blamed for reflecting flaws
on the face; objective laws are not to be blamed for
showing the mistakes made by man.

—Hanfeizi by Han Fei (c.280 – 233BC), legalist
and statesman of late Warring States Period

Terms:
a. 見：同"現"，顯現 to show
b. 疵（cī）：瑕疵；缺點 spots on jade, a metaphor for flaws
c. 道：規律 objective laws
d. 明：使……顯現 to show

5. 貌言華也，至言實也，苦言藥也，甘言疾也。

——《史記‧商君列傳》

Polite words are flowers, honest words are fruit, jarring
words are medicine, but sweet words lead to trouble.

—Historical Records by Sima Qian (c.145 or 135 – ? BC)
of the Han Dynasty

Terms:
a. 貌言：客氣話 polite words
b. 華：花 flowers
c. 至言：中肯的話 honest words
d. 實：果實 fruit
e. 疾：病；禍患 trouble; calamities

七、 人倫關係
Human Relations

1. 非我而當者，吾師也；是我而當者，吾友也；
諂諛我者，吾賊也。 ——《荀子‧修身》

He who criticizes me and correctly is my teacher; he who approves of me and correctly is my friend; he who flatters me does harm to me.

—Xunzi by Xun Kuang (313 – 238 BC), thinker and educator of the Warring States Period

Terms:
a. 非我：認為我不對，引伸為 "批評我" to criticize me
b. 當 (dàng)：恰當 correctly
c. 是我：認為我正確 to regard me as correct
d. 諂諛 (chǎn yú)：奉承 to flatter
e. 賊：害人之人 one who harms others

2. 以權利合者，權利盡而交疏。 ——《史記‧鄭世家》

Friends based on power and wealth get alienated when power is lost and wealth spent.

—Historical Records by Sima Qian (c.145 or 135 – ? BC) of the Han Dynasty

Terms:
a. 權：權力 power
b. 利：財力 wealth

3.　詳交者不失人，泛結者多後悔。　　——《抱朴子・交際》

Those who are prudent in making friends will not make false friends; those who are indiscreet in making friends will regret often.

—Baopuzi by Ge Hong (284 – 364) of the East Jin Dynasty

Terms:
a.　詳交：慎重交友 be prudent in making friends
b.　失人：交錯朋友 to make false friends
c.　泛結：濫交 be indiscreet in making friends

4.　海內存知己，天涯若比鄰。

　　　　　　　　——唐・王勃《送杜少府之任蜀州》

Since I have a bosom friend like you in the world, even if you are at the end of the earth, we still feel like next-door neighbours.

—Wang Bo (650 – 676), writer of the Tang Dynasty

Terms:
a.　海內：四海之內 in this world
b.　存：有 to have
c.　天涯：遙遠的地方 the remote end of the earth
d.　比鄰：近鄰 close neighbours

Note:
This is from a poem by the poet seeing a friend off to a distant place.

5.　君子之於天下也，無適也，無莫也，義之與比。

　　　　　　　　　　　　　——《論語・里仁》

In dealing with the people of the country, the ruler (or an honourable man) should not be close to some and indifferent to others. He should only keep terms with the righteous people.

—The Analects, a Confucian classic recording the words and deeds of Confucius and his dialogues with his disciples

Terms:

a. 適（dí）：親厚 to be close to
b. 莫：疏薄 to alienate
c. 比（bì）：親近 to keep terms with
d. 君子：西周、春秋時對貴族的通稱，指當時的統治階級；春秋末年以後，"君子"逐漸指"有德者" During the Western Zhou (1046 – 256 BC) and the Spring and Autumn Period (722 – 481), *Junzi* referred to the ruling class; since the end of the Spring and Autumn Period, it has been used to refer to people of virtuous character.

6. 落地為兄弟，何必骨肉親！

—— 晉・陶淵明《雜詩》十二首之一

People are brothers and sisters the moment they are born, so why does it have to be ties of kindred?

—Tao Yuanming (365 – 427), poet of the Jin Dynasty

Terms:

落地：降生 as soon as one is born

7. 四海之內，皆兄弟也。   —— 《論語・顏淵》

All the people within the four seas (or within the country) are brothers.

—The Analects, a Confucian classic recording the words and deeds of Confucius and his dialogues with his disciples

Terms:

四海：全國 within the four seas; within the country

8. 以財交者，財盡而交絕；以色交者，華落而愛渝。

——《戰國策·楚策》

Friendship based on wealth will come to an end when wealth is spent; love based on good looks will vanish when good looks fades away.

—Strategies of the Warring States compiled Liu Xiang
(c.77 – 6 BC) of the Western Han Dynasty

Terms:
a. 色：姿色；容貌 good looks
b. 華落：光彩消失 when good looks fade away
c. 渝：變 to change; to vanish

9. 水至清則無魚，人至察則無徒。

——《大戴禮記·子張問入官》

When the water is crystal clear, there is no fish in it; when a man is sharply observant, he has no friends with him.

—Da Dai's Book of Rites compiled by Dai De,
scholar on rites of the Western Han Dynasty

Terms:
a. 至：過於 excessively
b. 察：明察 observant
c. 徒：朋友 friends

10. 君子贈人以言，庶人贈人以財。　　——《荀子·大略》

When bidding farewell to friends, honourable people offer advice and ordinary people offer money.

—Xunzi by Xun Kuang (313 – 238 BC), thinker
and educator of the Warring States Period

Terms:
庶人：普通人 ordinary people

11. 君子不盡人之歡，不竭人之忠，以全交也。

——《禮記‧曲禮上》

An honourable man does not exhaust people's feelings toward him, or wear out their loyalty to him, so that their friendship can continue.

—The Book of Rites, a Confucian classic

Terms:
a. 盡：用盡 to exhaust
b. 歡：對人的盛情 feelings
c. 竭：用盡 to wear out

12. 不惜歌者苦，但傷知音稀。

——漢‧無名氏《古詩十九首》之五

It's not that I pity the singer's heartache, but I am sad that few listeners understand his songs.

—Collection of 19 Poems by anonymous poet(s)
of the Han Dynasty

Terms:
a. 惜：同情 to pity
b. 傷：難過 sad

13. 誰謂古今殊，異代可同調。

——南朝‧宋‧謝靈運《七里瀨》

Who says the past differs from the present? People in different times can have similar interest.

—Xie Lingyun (385 – 433), poet of the
State of Song of the Southern Dynasties

Terms:
a. 殊（shū）：不同 to differ; be different
b. 同調：志趣相同 to have the same interest

14. 志合者不以山海為遠，道乖者不以咫尺為近。

——《抱朴子・博喻》

People of similar interest do not consider the distance of seas and mountains as far; people of different beliefs do not consider the distance of one foot as near.

—Baopuzi by Ge Hong (284 – 364) of the East Jin Dynasty

Terms:
a. 道乖（guāi）者：信仰不合的人；主張相違的人 people of different beliefs
b. 咫尺：一尺的距離 the distance of one foot

15. 道不同，不相為謀。　　　　——《論語・衛靈公》

People of different beliefs do not seek / take counsel from each other.

—The Analects, a Confucian classic recording the words and deeds of Confucius and his dialogues with his disciples

Terms:
道：主張 views; beliefs

16. 志道者少友，逐俗者多儔。　——漢・王符《潛夫論・實貢》

People committed to moral principles and lofty ideals do not have many friends; those who drift along with the tide have many partners.

—Social Evils through the Eye of a Hermit by Wang Fu (c.85 – 162), philosopher of the Eastern Han Dynasty

Terms:

a. 志道者：有節操、有理想的人 people who are committed to moral principles and lofty ideals

b. 儔（chóu）：伙伴 partners

17. 我有旨酒，與汝樂之。　　——晉·陶淵明《答龐參軍》其三

I have some mellow wine, and I'd like to share it with you.

—Tao Yuanming (365 – 427), poet of the Jin Dynasty

Terms:

a. 旨酒：美酒 mellow wine

b. 汝：你 you

18. 同聲相應，同氣相求。　　——《周易·乾·文言》

Sounds of the same tune echo each other; people of the same character look for each other.

—The Book of Changes, a Confucian classic

八、思想感情
Ideas and Feelings

（一）愛國情懷
Patriotism

1. **苟利國家生死以，豈因禍福避趨之！**

    —— 清・林則徐《赴戍登程口占示家人》

    If it is in the interest of the country, I am ready to sacrifice my life;
    there is no reason to keep away from misfortune or pursue good fortune.

    —Lin Zexu (1785 – 1850) of the Qing Dynasty

    Terms:
    a. 苟：如果 if
    b. 生死：偏指 "死" life and death, with emphasis on death
    c. 生死以：死也心甘 ready to die
    d. 趨：追求 to seek

    Note:
    Lin Zexu (1785 – 1850) was governor-general of Hunan and Hubei of the Qing Dynasty. After the Opium War broke out, he reinforced defence along the coast against the British forces. However, he was framed and persecuted by the capitulators and removed from office. Soon he was banished to Xinjiang in the far northwest. This couplet is from a poem he composed orally when he was bidding farewell to his family.

2. 落紅不是無情物，化作春泥更護花。

—— 清·龔自珍《己亥雜詩》之五

Fallen flowers are not without feelings, for they can still protect the roots of the plant when melted and mixed up with spring mud.

—Gong Zizhen (1792 – 1841), poet of late Qing Dynasty

Terms:

a. 落紅：落花 fallen flowers
b. 更：還 still

Note:

Gong Zizhen was a thinker and writer of the Qing Dynasty. These two lines are from a poem he wrote after he resigned from office in Beijing and went back home in Hangzhou in 1839.

3. 位卑未敢忘憂國，事定猶須待闔棺。

—— 宋·陸游《病起書懷》

Though I'm in a humble position, I dare not neglect to worry about the destiny of the country, and I'll not stop worrying until the cover of the coffin is nailed up.

—Lu You (1125 – 1210), poet of the Southern Song Dynasty

Terms:

a. 位卑：地位低下 humble status
b. 事定：指憂國憂民的思想停止 when I stop worrying about the destiny of the state
c. 闔 (hé)：蓋上棺蓋，指"死" until the cover of the coffin is nailed up, meaning when he died

4. 閑居非吾志，甘心赴國憂。　—— 三國·魏·曹植《雜詩》

It is not my wish to stay idle at home, I am ready to go tackling the crisis for the country.

—Cao Zhi (192 – 232), poet of the State of Wei of the Three Kingdoms

Terms:
a. 赴：走進 to go into; to tackle
b. 國憂：國難 national crisis

5. 有葡萄美酒，芙蓉寶劍，都未稱平生志。

—— 清・文廷式《水龍吟》

Neither grape wine nor lotus swords can fulfill my
life's ambition.

—Wen Tingshi (1856 – 1904), scholar of the Qing Dynasty

Terms:
a. 芙蓉：荷花 lotus
b. 稱（chèn）：滿足 to satisfy; to fulfill

6. 少日功名空自許，今老矣，欲何如？

—— 金・段成己《江城子》

When I was young, I aspired to an official career in
vain; but now, what shall I do when I am turning an
old man?

—Duan Chengji (1199 – 1279) of the Jin Dynasty

Terms:
a. 少日：少年時 when young
b. 自許：自命 to aspire to

7. 書生老去雄圖在，不信江湖有棄才。

—— 清・喻長霖《再遊南鸞》

This scholar is getting old, but he still cherishes lofty
aspirations, for he does not believe that a capable man
should be rejected by the world.

—Yu Changlin (1857 – 1940) of the Qing Dynasty

Terms:

a. 雄圖：遠大抱負 great ambitions; lofty aspirations

b. 江湖：泛指世界 the world

8. 休言女子非英物，夜夜龍泉壁上鳴。

———清‧秋瑾《鷓鴣天》

Do not say women cannot be heroines; every night my Longquan sword rings on the wall.

—Qiu Jin (1879 – 1907) of the Qing Dynasty

Terms:

a. 英物：英雄 heroine

b. 龍泉：龍泉寶劍 *Longquan* sword

Note:

Qiu Jin was an advocator of women's right and a revolutionary martyr to the cause of overthrowing the Qing Dynasty.

（二）壯志凌雲
Soaring Ambitions

1. 燕雀安知鴻鵠之志哉！

———《史記‧陳涉世家》

A swallow or a sparrow can never understand the lofty ambitions of a swan.

—Historical Records by Sima Qian (c.145 or 135 – ? BC) of the Han Dynasty

Terms:

鴻鵠 (hóng hú)：天鵝 swan

2. 老驥伏櫪，志在千里；烈士暮年，壯心不已。

—— 漢·曹操《龜雖壽》

The old steed over the manger still has the mind to
do a thousand-*li* journey; the heroic old man still
cherishes lofty ambitions.

—*Cao Cao (155 – 220), statesman and poet*
of the State of Wei of the Three Kingdoms

Terms:

a. 驥：駿馬 steed
b. 櫪：馬槽 a manger
c. 烈士：有志建立功業的人 a man ready to achieve feats

3. 寧與黃鵠比翼乎？將與雞鶩爭食乎？

—— 戰國·楚·屈原《卜居》

Would you rather soar up into the sky and race with
the swans? Or would you prefer to team up with the
chicks and ducks and vie with them for food?

—*Qu Yuan (c.340 – 277 BC), minister and poet*
of the State of Chu of the Warring States Period

Terms:

a. 黃鵠：天鵝 swan
b. 雞鶩：雞鴨 chicks and ducks

4. 十年磨一劍，霜刃未曾試。
今日把示君，誰有不平事？　　　—— 唐·賈島《劍客》

It has taken ten years to grind the sword,
Its edges, casting cold light, have not been tested yet.
Now let me take it out for you to have a look,
In case anybody has a grievance to address.

—*"The Swordsman" by Jia Dao (779 – 843), poet of the Tang Dynasty*

Terms:
a. 霜刃：白刃 edges that cast cold light
b. 把示：拿出來讓你看 to take out for you to see
c. 不平事：委屈；牢騷 grievances

5. 天生我材必有用，千金散盡還復來。

——唐・李白《將進酒》

Since Heaven has brought me to the world, I must
　　have my own usefulness.
When the thousand pieces of gold are spent, they'll
　　come back to me sooner or later.

—Li Bai (701 – 762), poet of the Tang Dynasty

6. 君子憂道不憂貧。　　　　　——《論語・衛靈公》

An honourable man worries about the lot of his
political doctrine, but not the poverty he suffers.

*—The Analects, a Confucian classic recording
the words and deeds of Confucius and his dialogues with his disciples*

Terms:
道：政治主張 political doctrine

7. 君子以致命遂志。　　　　　——《周易・困・象》

An honourable man can sacrifice his life for his ideal.

—The Book of Changes, a Confucian classic

Terms:
a. 致命：捨棄生命 to sacrifice one's life
b. 遂志：實現志向；實現理想 to realize one's ideal; to realize what
one advocates

8.　丈夫為志，窮當益堅，老當益壯。

——《後漢書・馬援列傳》

When a true man makes up his mind to fulfill his lofty
ideal, he should be all the more determined when
under adverse circumstances, and all the more valiant
when getting on in years.

—History of Eastern Han by Fan Ye (398 – 445), historian
of the State of Song of the Southern Dynasties

Terms:

a. 丈夫：大丈夫；有志氣的人 a true man with lofty ideals
b. 窮：困窘 be under adverse circumstances
c. 益：更加 all the more

（三）思人
Missing the Dear Ones

1.　可憐無定河邊骨，猶是春閨夢裏人。

——唐・陳陶《隴西行》

How grief-stricken that the white bones lying along
　　the Wuding River,
Belong to the soldiers who still live
　　in the dreams of their wives at home.

—Chen Tao, poet of the Tang Dynasty

Terms:

a. 無定河：黃河一支流，在陝西北部 a tributary of the Yellow River
in the north of Shaanxi Province
b. 春閨：古代女子的閨房 young women's chamber, metaphor for
the wives of soldiers fighting on frontiers

2. 獨在異鄉為異客，每逢佳節倍思親。

── 唐・王維《九月九日憶山東兄弟》

Living away from home as a solitary stranger,
I miss my folks all the more on festive occasions.

—*Wang Wei (701 – 761; 698 – 759), poet of the Tang Dynasty*

3. 君自故鄉來，應知故鄉事。
來日綺窗前，寒梅著花未？

── 唐・王維《雜詩》三首之二

Since you've come from our hometown,
You should know what's happening there.
Was the plum in front of the fancy window
Coming into flower when you left?

—*Wang Wei (701 – 761; 698 – 759), poet of the Tang Dynasty*

Terms:
a. 綺（qǐ）窗：舊時女子居住的房間的窗戶，多有裝飾 decorated windows of women's chambers
b. 著（zhuó）花：開花 (of flowers) to bloom

4. 馬上相逢無紙筆，憑君傳語報平安。

── 唐・岑參《逢入京使》

Since we meet on horseback and I have no paper and
   writing brush,
Please take a message home and tell my folks that I'm
   fine over here.

—*Cen Shen (c.714 – 770), poet of the Tang Dynasty*

Note:
When the poet wrote this poem from which these two lines are taken he was in Anxi, about ten thousand *li* from his home in Chang'an, capital of the Tang Dynasty.

5. 烽火連三月，家書抵萬金。　　　　　——唐・杜甫《春望》

With the war dragging on for three months running,
A letter from home is worth ten thousand pieces of
gold.

—Du Fu (712 – 770), poet of the Tang Dynasty

Terms:
a. 烽火：指戰爭 war
b. 家書：家信 letter to or from home

（四）思鄉
Homesickness

1. 寄言此日南征雁，一到春來早北歸。

——清・顧炎武《懷人》

Let me entrust a message to the wild geese heading
　　southward,
Please return to the north as soon as spring comes.

—Gu Yanwu (1613 – 1682), scholar and thinker
of late Ming and early Qing Dynasty

Terms:
寄言：帶消息給人 to have a message taken to

Note:
The poet badly misses someone in the south and is anxious to
hear from him or her, but it is not known who was the person he
misses.

2. 悲莫悲兮生別離，樂莫樂兮新相知。

—— 戰國・屈原《九歌・少司命》

Oh, sad indeed, but nothing is sadder than when you
have to part from your dear ones;
Oh, happy indeed, but nothing is happier than when
you first make your bosom friends.

*—Qu Yuan (c.340 – 277 BC), minister and poet
of the State of Chu of the Warring States Period*

3. 春風又綠江南岸，明月何時照我還？

—— 宋・王安石《泊船瓜洲》

Once again spring breeze brings green to the south of
the Yangtze River,
But when can I go home with the moon shining all the
way?

*—Wang Anshi (1021 – 1086), statesman, thinker
and writer of the Northern Song Dynasty*

Terms:
綠 (lǜ)：形容詞用作動詞，變綠 to become green

4. 雲橫秦嶺家何在，雪擁藍關馬不前。

—— 唐・韓愈《左遷至藍關示姪孫湘》

With Mt. Qinling overcast by thick clouds, I wondered
where my home was;
With Languan enveloped by heavy snows, the horse
hesitated to go forward.

*—Han Yu (768 – 824), writer and
philosopher of the Tang Dynasty*

Terms:

a. 秦嶺：陝西境內山脈 a mountain range in Shaanxi Province

b. 藍關：陝西境內地名 a place in Shaanxi Province

5.　鳥飛反故鄉兮，狐死必首丘。

—— 戰國・楚・屈原《九章・哀郢》

1) Birds will return to their home place,
　　no matter how far away they fly;
　Foxes will point their heads toward the mounds
　　when they are dying.

2) Birds flying away will return to their home place,
　Foxes when dying point their heads toward the
　mounds.

*—Qu Yuan (c.340 – 277 BC), minister and poet
of the State of Chu of the Warring States Period*

Terms:

a. 反：通"返" to return

b. 首丘：使頭朝向土丘 to point the head toward the mound

Note:

Qu Yuan, the great poet and minister of the State of Chu, was exiled after he had fallen out of favour with the prince. Later, Yingdu, Chu's capital, was conquered by the State of Qin. That prompted him to write the poem "Elegy to Ying" by which he expressed his deep grief and indignation. These two lines quoted here metaphorically express his melancholy love for his country and its capital.

（五）別情
Part with Emotions and Return with Mixed Feelings

1. 勸君更盡一杯酒，西出陽關無故人。

—— 唐・王維《送元二使安西》

Let me propose one more toast to you, my comrade,
You'll have no friends west of the Yangguan Pass.

—*Wang Wei (701 – 761; 698 – 759), poet of the Tang Dynasty*

Terms:
a. 更盡一杯酒：再喝一杯酒 to drink up another cup of wine
b. 陽關：古代關口，在甘肅玉門關之南 an ancient pass in Gansu, the passage out to the west in ancient China

2. 少小離家老大回，鄉音無改鬢毛衰。
兒童相見不相識，笑問客從何處來。

—— 唐・賀知章《回鄉偶書》

I went away from home a child, and come back an old
   man,
My native accent unchanged, but my temples have
   turned grey.
When the kids in the village find me a stranger,
They ask with a smile, "Where are you coming from,
   sir?"

—*He Zhizhang (659 – 744), poet of the Tang Dynasty*

3. 近鄉情更怯，不敢問來人。　　—— 唐・李頻《渡漢江》

The nearer I get to my home village, the more timid I
become, and so I dare not ask the villager I meet about
my folks.

—Li Pin (818 – 876), poet of the Tang Dynasty

4. 請君試問東流水，別意與之誰短長。

—— 唐・李白《金陵酒肆留別》

Please go and ask the eastward water of the Yangtze
River, as compared with the sorrow of parting, which
is longer and which is shorter.

—Li Bai (701 – 762), poet of the Tang Dynasty

九、思想方法
Way of Thinking

（一）審時度勢
Take Stock of Situations

1. 時止則止，時行則行。 ——《周易・艮・象》

When it's time to halt, halt; when it's time to act, act.

—The Book of Changes, a Confucian classic

Terms:
時：時機 when it's time to do something

2. 得時則昌，失時則亡。 ——《尹文子・大道上》

When you go in harmony with the trend of times,
you thrive; when you go against the trend of times,
you perish.

—YinWenzi by Yin Wen of the Warring States Period

Terms:
a. 時：時勢 the trend of times
b. 昌：昌盛 to thrive

3. 勇者不避難，智者不失時。 ——《史記・仲尼弟子列傳》

Courageous people do not shun danger and crises, and
wise people do not miss opportunities.

*—Historical Records by Sima Qian (c.145
or 135 – ? BC) of the Han Dynasty*

4. 天下理無常是，事無常非。　　　　——《列子·説符篇》

In this world, what is true may not be always true,
and what is false may not be always false.

—Liezi, Taoist classical work by Lie Yukou of the Warring States Period

Terms:
a. 常：永遠 always
b. 是：正確 right; true
c. 非：錯誤 wrong; false

5. 雖有智慧，不如乘勢；雖有鎡基，不如待時。

——《孟子·公孫丑上》

Though you have wisdom, it's more advisable to take
advantage of favourable situations; though you have a
hoe, it's more advisable to wait for the right season.

—Mencius by Meng Ke (c.372 – 289 BC), philosopher
and Confucian scholar of the Warring States Period

Terms:
a. 乘勢：抓住有利時機 to take advantage of favourable situations
b. 鎡 (zī) 基：鋤頭 hoe

6. 事之難易，不在小大，務在知時。

——《呂氏春秋·首時》

The extent of difficulty does not lie in the size of the
business; it depends on timely grasp of opportunities.

—Lü's Spring and Autumn Annuals, compiled under the
sponsorship of Lü Buwei, Prime Minister of the State
of Qin during the late Warring States Period

（二）自知之明
View Oneself in Perspective

1. 敗莫大於不自知。　　　　　——《呂氏春秋·自知》

Failure is caused, more than anything else, by lack of proper self-assessment.

—Lü's Spring and Autumn Annuals, compiled under the sponsorship of Lü Buwei, Prime Minister of the State of Qin during the late Warring States Period

2. 欲知人，必須自知。　　　　　——《鬼谷子·反應》

If you want to know / understand others, you must know / understand yourself first.

—Guiguzi by Guiguzi of the State of Chu during the Warring States Period

3. 以五十步笑百步。　　　　　——《孟子·梁惠王上》

Those who have fled fifty paces laugh at those who have fled one hundred paces.

—Mencius by Meng Ke (c.372 – 289 BC), philosopher and Confucian scholar of the Warring States Period

Comment: These are the people who cannot understand themselves.

十、教育與學習
Education and Study

（一）學習態度
Attitude towards Study

1. 知人無務，不若愚而好學。 ——《淮南子·修務訓》

Intelligent people who do not study hard are not as praiseworthy as slow-witted people who are hard-working in studying.

—Huainanzi by Prince Huainan Liu An (179 – 122 BC)
and some of his followers of the Western Han Dynasty

Terms:
a. 知：通 "智" intelligent
b. 無務：不努力學習 not work hard

2. 學進於振而廢於窮。 ——漢·王符《潛夫論·贊學》

Learning flourishes with persistent effort and declines when neglected.

—Social Evils through the Eye of a Hermit by Wang Fu
(c.85 – 162), philosopher of the Eastern Han Dynasty

Terms:
a. 振：奮發 by making feverish effort
b. 窮：止；荒廢 to be neglected

3. 學而不已，闔棺乃止。　　　　　——《韓詩外傳》卷八

There is no end of learning until one is encased in coffin.

*—Collection of Comments on Ancient Affairs with Quotes from
The Book of Songs by Han Ying of the Western Han Dynasty*

Terms:

闔（hé）：蓋上 to encase (a coffin)

4. 百川到東海，何時復西歸？
少壯不努力，老大徒傷悲。　　　——漢・無名氏《長歌行》

All rivers flow into the East Sea.
They never flow back to the west.
If you do not work hard when young,
It's no use crying over spilt milk when old.

—An anonymous poet of the Han Dynasty

5. 讀書破萬卷，下筆如有神。
　　　　　　　　—— 唐・杜甫《奉贈韋左丞丈二十二韻》

When you have read over ten thousand books, you can
write like divine-inspired / magic.

—Du Fu (712 – 770), poet of the Tang Dynasty

Terms:

破：超過 more than

6. 人一能之，己百之；人十能之，己千之。
果能此道矣，雖愚必明，雖柔必強。

——《禮記‧中庸》

If others can do it by making one effort, I will do
it by making one hundred efforts; if others can do
it by making ten efforts, I will do it by making one
thousand efforts. If one can apply himself this way,
the slow-witted can become quick-witted, and the
weak can become the strong.

—The Book of Rites, a Confucian classic

7. 不能則學，疑則問。　　　——《大戴禮記‧曾子制言上》

1) If there is anything you cannot do, learn to do it; if
   there is anything you are not sure of, ask about it.
2) Learn to do what you are incapable of and enquire
   about what you are not sure of.

—Da Dai's Book of Rites compiled by Dai De,
scholar on rites of the Western Han Dynasty

8. 君子取人貴恕，及論學術，則不得不嚴。

—— 清‧方東樹《昭昧詹言》

An honourable man should be generous and forgiving
to others, but when it comes to scholarship, he has to
maintain a strict standard.

—Fang Dongshu, scholar of the Qing Dynasty

9. 不興其藝，不能樂學。　　　　——《禮記‧學記》

1) If you are not interested in what you are learning, you will not enjoy the learning of it.
2) If you do not relish what you are learning, you feel no delight in it.

—The Book of Rites, a Confucian classic

Terms:

a. 興（xìng）：喜歡 to be interested; to relish
b. 藝：指所學的東西 what you learn

10. 無冥冥之志者，無昭昭之明；無惛惛之事者，無赫赫之功。　　　　——《荀子‧勸學》

If you do not devote yourself to what you do, you cannot have a thorough understanding of it; if you do not apply yourself to your undertaking, you cannot accomplish anything notable.

—Xunzi by Xun Kuang (313 – 238 BC), thinker and educator of the Warring States Period

Terms:

a. 冥冥（míng）：專心致志 to devote oneself to
b. 昭昭（zhāo）：明白 understanding
c. 惛惛（hūn）：義同 "冥冥" to apply oneself to
d. 赫赫（hè）：顯著的 prominent; notable

11. 古之學者為己，今之學者為人。　　——《論語‧憲問》

Ancient learners studied to improve themselves (or enlarge their own knowledge), but today's learners study to flaunt their knowledge.

—The Analects, a Confucian classic recording the words and deeds of Confucius and his dialogues with his disciples

Terms:

a. 學者：學習者 learners

b. 為人：向人顯示；炫耀 to flaunt to others

12. 好讀書，不求甚解。　　——晉・陶淵明《五柳先生傳》

He takes delight in reading, but he does not read for thorough understanding (or bother about minor details).

—Tao Yuanming (365 – 427), poet of the Jin Dynasty

Terms:

a. 好（hào）：喜歡 to like

b. 不求甚解：不求透徹理解 not bother about minor details

13. 萬卷山積，一篇吟成。　　——清・袁枚《續詩品・博習》

1) It is only after I have read ten thousand books piled up like a mountain that I have been able to come up with one poem.

2) It is only after I have read heaps of books that I have been able to write one poem.

—Yuan Mei (1716 – 1798), poet of the Qing Dynasty

（二）教與學
Teach and Learn

1.   學而時習之，不亦説乎？   ——《論語・學而》

1) Isn't it a delightful thing to constantly apply what you've learned?
2) Isn't it a pleasurable experience to constantly review what you have learned?

> —*The Analects, a Confucian classic recording the words and deeds of Confucius and his dialogues with his disciples*

Terms:
a. 習：應用；複習 to apply; to review
b. 説（yuè）：通"悦"，快樂 delightful

2.   學其上，僅得其中；學其中，斯為下矣。

——   宋・嚴羽《滄浪詩話・詩辯》

In studying, if you set a high standard, you can only get to the medium; if you set a medium standard, you can only get to the low.

> —*Yan Yu, literary critic of the Southern Song Dynasty*

Comment: One should always set a high standard in studying.

3.   學如牛毛，成如麟角。

——北齊・顏之推《顏氏家訓・養生》

1) There are too many people studying, but few have succeeded.
2) Too many people are studying, but very few are successful.

> —*Admonitions of the Yan's Family by Yan Zhitui (531 – 590) of the Northern Qi Dynasty*

Terms:
a. 牛毛：形容很多 too many
b. 麟角：形容很少 few

4. 蠶食桑而所吐者絲，非桑也；蜂採花，
而所釀者蜜非花。　　—— 清・袁枚《隨園詩話》卷十三

1) Silkworms eat mulberry leaves, but spit out silk
instead; honey bees sip at flowers to collect nectar,
but they make honey instead.
2) Silkworms eat mulberry leaves, but what they spit
out is silk, not mulberry leaves; honey bees sip at
flowers to collect nectar, but what they make is
honey, not flowers.

—Yuan Mei (1716 – 1798), poet of the Qing Dynasty

5. 幼而學者，如日出之光；老而學者，如秉燭夜行。

—— 北齊・顏之推《顏氏家訓・勉學》

To begin studying from childhood is like the rising
sun radiating brilliant light; to begin studying in old
age is like walking at night with a candle light.

—Admonitions of the Yan's Family by Yan Zhitui
(531 – 590) of the Northern Qi Dynasty

6. 有書堆數仞，不如讀盈寸。　　—— 清・劉岩《雜詩》

To possess a collection of books piled dozens of feet
high is not as meaningful as read one inch of them.

—Liu Yan of the Qing Dynasty

Terms:
仞（rèn）：古代長度單位，約為八尺 ancient unit of length, about ten
feet or so

7. 逸居而無教，則近於禽獸。　　——《孟子‧滕文公上》

If one lives in ease and comfort without education, he is no more than an animal.

— Mencius by Meng Ke (c.372 – 289 BC), philosopher and Confucian scholar of the Warring States Period

Terms:

a. 逸居：生活安樂 to live in ease and comfort

b. 教：教育 education

8. 學者非必為仕，而仕者必如學。　　——《荀子‧大略》

1) When you study, you don't have to be an official; but if you are an official, you must study.

2) When you read, you do not read in order to take office; but if you have taken office, you must read.

— Xunzi by Xun Kuang (313 – 238 BC), thinker and educator of the Warring States Period

Comment: Scholars don't have to be government officials, but government officials must read to refine their temperament and enlarge their knowledge.

9. 盡信《書》，則不如無《書》。　　——《孟子‧盡心下》

If you trust *Shangshu* without reserve, you had better go without it.

— Mencius by Meng Ke (c.372 – 289 BC), philosopher and Confucian scholar of the Warring States Period

Terms:

《書》：《尚書》，或《書經》 *Shangshu*, Collection of Ancient Texts

Comment: Read and think rather than rely on books blindly.

10. 遺子黃金滿籯，不如一經。 　　——《漢書·韋賢傳》

1) To bequeath your children a basketful of gold is not as good as give them Confucian classics to study.
2) It's better to leave your children books to study than bequeath them a basketful of gold to live on.

—History of Han, chronicle of the Han Dynasty between 206 BC and 23 AD by Ban Gu (32 – 92)

Terms:

a. 遺：留給 to bequeath
b. 籯（yíng）：筐之類的器具 basket
c. 經：儒家經典，泛指書籍 Confucian classics; books

（三）從師
Learn from the Teacher

1. 三人行，必有我師焉。 　　——《論語·述而》

1) When I am in the company of two others, I can always find something to learn from them.
2) In the company of two others, I can always find one worthy of being my teacher.

—The Analects, a Confucian classic recording the words and deeds of Confucius and his dialogues with his disciples

2. 學莫便乎近其人。 　　——《荀子·勸學》

The best way to learn is to keep close to a good teacher.

—Xunzi by Xun Kuang (313 – 238 BC), thinker and educator of the Warring States Period

Terms:

a. 便：適宜 the best way; the proper way

b. 其人：良師 a good teacher; a good instructor

Comment: The advantage of keeping close to a good teacher is to facilitate learning from his moral conduct as well as knowledge.

3. 凡學之道，嚴師為難。師嚴，然後道尊。
   道尊，然後民知敬學。　　　　　——《禮記·學記》

With regard to study, the most difficult thing is to heighten respect for the teacher. Once the teacher is respected, Confucian doctrine is held in high esteem. Once Confucian doctrine is held in high esteem, the people will study it in earnest.

—The Book of Rites, a Confucian classic

Terms:
a. 凡學之道：關於學習 with regard to study
b. 嚴：尊敬 to respect
c. 道尊：這裏的 "道" 指儒家主張 Confucian doctrine

4. 國將興，必貴師而重傅……國將衰，必賤師而輕傅。

　　　　　　　　　　　　　　　——《荀子·大略》

When the country is going to flourish, teachers are sure to be respected ... When the country is going to decline, teachers are sure to be disrespected.

—Xunzi by Xun Kuang (313 – 238 BC), thinker
and educator of the Warring States Period

Terms:
a. 貴師：以老師為貴，尊崇老師 to respect teachers
b. 重傅：重視老師 to respect teachers
c. 賤師：輕視老師 to disrespect teachers
d. 輕傅：輕視老師 to disrespect teachers

（四）教師
Teacher

1. 溫故而知新，可以為師矣。　　　——《論語・為政》

If one can attain new understanding by reviewing (or out of) old knowledge, he can qualify as a teacher.

—The Analects, a Confucian classic recording the words and deeds of Confucius and his dialogues with his disciples

Terms:
a. 溫故：複習舊知識 to review old knowledge
b. 知新：有新體會 to attain new understanding; to add new dimensions to understanding

2. 學然後知不足，教然後知困。　　　——《禮記・學記》

Study makes one realize his inadequacy; teaching makes one realize that there are still things he does not know.

—The Book of Rites, a Confucian classic

Terms:
a. 不足：不夠 inadequacy; weakness
b. 困：有所不通 not well versed in certain aspects of the knowledge concerned

3. 君子之于子也，愛而勿面也，使而勿貌也，
導之以道而勿強也。　　　——《大戴禮記・曾子立事》

In relation to his children, an honourable man can love them, but he must not have his love written in his face; he can make them work, but he must not externalize his intent; he can reason with them, but he must not force them to do what they are not up to.

—*Da Dai's Book of Rites compiled by Dai De,*
scholar on rites of the Western Han Dynasty

Terms:

a. 之于子也：對於子女 in relation to one's children

b. 面：表現在臉上 to externalize

c. 使：支使 to make somebody work

d. 貌：義同 "面"，表現在臉上 to externalize

e. 強（qiǎng）：強迫 to force

4. 有教無類。   ——《論語·衛靈公》

1) Education should not discriminate between classes.

2) Education should not discriminate in favour of some and against others.

—*The Analects, a Confucian classic recording the words and*
deeds of Confucius and his dialogues with his disciples

5. 君子正身以俟，欲來者不距，欲去者不止。

——《荀子·法行》

An honourable man preserves his personal integrity and wait for people to come for instructions. Anyone willing to come is not refused, and anyone intending to go is not stopped.

—*Xunzi by Xun Kuang (313 – 238 BC), thinker*
and educator of the Warring States Period

Terms:

a. 俟（sì）：等待 to wait

b. 距：通 "拒"，拒絕 to refuse

c. 止：阻止 to stop

十一、惜時
Cherish Time

1. 盛年不重來，一日難再晨。
及時當勉勵，歲月不待人。

—— 晉‧陶淵明《雜詩》十二首之一

The exuberant years of life will not return,
The morning of the day does not repeat itself.
Seize your time and brace yourself up,
For time does not stop to wait for you.

—Tao Yuanming (365 – 427), poet of the Jin Dynasty

2. 青春須早為，豈能長少年！

—— 唐‧孟郊《勸學》

Do something worthy while you are young, for youth does not stay long.

—Meng Jiao (751 – 814), poet of the Tang Dynasty

3. 少則志一而難忘，長則神放而易失。

——《抱朴子‧勖學》

As a child's mind is focused, he is not apt to forget what he learns; as an adult's mind is divided, what he has learned easily escapes his memory.

—Baopuzi by Ge Hong (284 – 364) of the East Jin Dynasty

Terms:

a. 志一：專一 concentrated; focused
b. 神放：精神分散 attention divided / distracted

4. 生也有涯，而知也無涯。 ———《莊子‧養生主》

1) Life is finite, but carnal desires are infinite.
2) Life is finite, but knowledge is infinite.

—Zhuangzi by Zhuang Zhou (c.369 – 286 BC)
and his followers of the Warring States Period

Terms:

a. 涯：盡頭 end; limit
b. 知 (zhì)：慾望；知識 carnal desires; knowledge

Note:

There is one interpretation of this quote that Taoists believe that one should restrain his carnal desires. Since life is finite and carnal desires infinite, there is no sense in making oneself constantly worried by seeking infinite desires with finite life. Later this " 知 " is used in the sense of "knowledge", meaning that since life is finite, one should do his best to learn as much knowledge as possible within his limited lifespan.

5. 聖人不貴尺之璧而重寸之陰，時難得而易失也。

———《淮南子‧原道訓》

A sage cherishes an inch of time instead of a foot of jade, because time is hard to attain and easy to lose.

—Huainanzi by Prince Huainan Liu An (179 – 122 BC)
and some of his followers of the Western Han Dynasty

Terms:

a. 尺之璧：一尺長的碧玉 a foot of jade
b. 寸之陰：一寸長的光陰 an inch of time

6. 子在川上曰："逝者如斯夫，不舍晝夜。"

——《論語・子罕》

The Master, standing by the river, said, "Time passes by like this, flowing away day and night."

—The Analects, a Confucian classic recording the words and deeds of Confucius and his dialogues with his disciples

Terms:
a. 逝者：指消失的時光 time passed
b. 斯：指流去的江水 the water flowing away in the river
c. 不舍晝夜：日夜不停 day and night

7. 去者日以疏，來者日以親。

——漢・無名氏《古詩十九首》之十四

The days gone by are fading further and further away, and old age is getting nearer day by day.

—Collection of 19 Poems by anonymous poet(s) of the Han Dynasty

Terms:
a. 去者：指已逝去的少年時光 the days gone by
b. 疏：遠去 getting far behind; fading away
c. 來者：指未來的暮年 old age that is approaching

8. 人生天地之間，若白駒之過郤，忽然而已。

——《莊子・知北遊》

The existence of man between heaven and earth is like a white colt bolting past a chink.

—Zhuangzi by Zhuang Zhou (c. 369 – 286 BC) and his followers of the Warring States Period

Terms:
郤（xì）：同"隙" a chink

9. 少年安得長少年，海波尚變為桑田。

——唐 • 李賀《嘲少年》

How can the young stay young for good,
Even oceans can become cropland.

—Li He (790 – 816), poet of the Tang Dynasty

10. 莫言三十是年少，百歲三分已一分。

——唐 • 白居易《花下自勸酒》

Don't say that one is still young at thirty,
Even if you live to be one hundred, one third of it is
    gone.

—Bai Juyi (772 – 846), poet of the Tang Dynasty

十二、養生
Preserve Health

1. 無憂者壽。 ——《抱朴子・道意》

A man free from worries is likely to enjoy a long life.

—*Baopuzi by Ge Hong (284 – 364) of the East Jin Dynasty*

2. 養心莫善於寡欲。 ——《孟子・盡心下》

The best way to breed your integrity is to remain free from worldly desires (or indifferent to worldly temptations).

—*Mencius by Meng Ke (c.372 – 289 BC), philosopher and Confucian scholar of the Warring States Period*

3. 能尊生者雖貴富不以養傷身，雖貧賤不以利累形。

——《莊子・讓王》

He who cherishes his life does not overindulge himself at the expense of his health, even if he lives in affluence and maintains an honourable position; nor does he wear himself out in order to net profit, even if he lives in poverty and ends up in a humble position.

—*Zhuangzi by Zhuang Zhou (c.369 – 286 BC) and his followers of the Warring States Period*

Terms:
a. 尊生：珍惜生命 to cherish one's life
b. 以養傷身：過度追求物質享受而傷害身體 to overindulge oneself at the expense of his health

c. 以利累形：為了謀取利益而勞累自己 to wear oneself out in order to get profit

4. 唯食忘憂。　　　　　　　——《左傳·昭公二十八年》

When you sit at table, forget what troubles you.

—Zuo Zhuan, first chronological history covering the period from 722 BC to 464 BC, attributed to Zuo Qiuming

Terms:

唯：句首助詞 a form word at the head of a sentence

5. 流水不腐，戶樞不螻，動也。　——《呂氏春秋·盡數》

Flowing water does not get rotten, because it keeps flowing; a door shaft does not get worm-eaten, because it keeps turning.

—Lü's Spring and Autumn Annuals, compiled under the sponsorship of Lü Buwei, Prime Minister of the State of Qin during the late Warring States Period

Terms:

戶樞：門軸 door shaft

十三、哲理
Philosophical Concepts

（一）轉化
Transformation

1. 日有短長，月有死生。 ──《孫子兵法·虛實篇》

The day is alternately long and short, and the moon is alternately full and curved.

—Master Sun's Art of War by Sun Bin, great military strategist of the late Spring and Autumn Period

Terms:

月有死生：指月有圓缺 the full moon and the curved moon

Note:

Sunzi's real name is Sun Wu. He is well-known for his masterwork of *The Art of War*.

2. 一晝一夜，華開者謝；一秋一春，物故者新。

── 明·劉基《司馬季主論卜》

Within a day and a night, flowers unfold and wither; from autumn to spring, the new grows out of the old.

—Liu Ji (1311 – 1375), minister of the Ming Dynasty

Terms:

a. 華：花 flowers

b. 故：舊 old

3. 秋早寒則冬必暖矣，春多雨則夏必旱矣。

——《呂氏春秋·情欲》

1) If autumn becomes cold early, winter will be warm;
if spring is rainy, summer will suffer from drought.
2) A cold autumn foretells (or is a sign of) a warm
winter and a rainy spring foretells (or is a sign of) a
drought in summer.

—Lü's Spring and Autumn Annuals, compiled under the
sponsorship of Lü Buwei, Prime Minister of the State
of Qin during the late Warring States Period

4. 朝華之草，夕而零落；松柏之茂，隆寒不衰。

——《三國志·魏書·王昶傳》

Grass that blooms in the morning withers in the
evening; exuberant pines and cypresses do not wilt
even in the depths of winter.

—History of the Three Kingdoms by Chen Shou
(233 – 297), historian of the Western Jin Dynasty

Terms:

a. 朝華之草：早晨開花的草 grass that blooms in the morning
b. 零落：凋落 to wither

（二）凡事有規律
Everything Has Its Own Course of Evolution

1.　物有必至，事有固然。　　　　——《史記·孟嘗君列傳》

　　1) Everything has its inevitable outcome, and
　　　　everything follows its own course of evolution.
　　2) Everything effects its inevitable outcome, and
　　　　everything has its own course to follow.

—Historical Records by Sima Qian (c.145
or 135 – ? BC) of the Han Dynasty

Terms:
a. 必至：必然結果 inevitable outcome
b. 固然：必然趨勢 its own course of evolution

2.　樹欲靜而風不止。　　　　——《韓詩外傳》卷九

The tree wants to keep still, but the wind doesn't stop
blowing.

—Collection of Comments on Ancient Affairs with Quotes
from The Book of Songs by Han Ying of the Western Han Dynasty

Comment: Objective law is independent of man's will.

3.　明於天人之分，則可謂至人矣。　　——《荀子·天論》

He who can distinguish between the law of nature and
the function of man is the most sensible man.

—Xunzi by Xun Kuang (313–238 BC), thinker
and educator of the Warring States Period

Terms:
a. 天人之分：自然規律和人的作用 the law of nature and the function
　 of man
b. 至人：最明白事理的人 the most sensible man

4. 晝風久，夜風止。   ——《孫子兵法・火攻篇》

When the wind blows for long during the day, it stops at night.

—Master Sun's Art of War by Sun Bin, great military
strategist of the late Spring and Autumn Period

5. 人便如此如此，天理不然不然。   ——《金瓶梅》

Although man tries to work things out this way or that way, the natural course of events does not go this way or that way.

—Plum in the Gold Vase, a novel
first published in early 17th century

6. 世有毋望之福，又有毋望之禍。

——《史記・春申君列傳》

In this world, there are unexpected fortunes and unexpected misfortunes as well.

—Historical Records by Sima Qian (c.145
or 135 – ? BC) of the Han Dynasty

Terms:
毋望：意外的 unexpected

7. 事有得而失，物有損而益。   ——唐・白居易《詠懷》

Sometimes there is loss in gain and sometimes there is gain in loss.

—Bai Juyi (772 – 846), poet of the Tang Dynasty

8. 使人無渡河可，使無波不可。　　　——《文子・上德》

You can tell people not to cross the river, but you cannot make the river waveless.

—Wenzi, a Taoist work by unknown author of the Warring States Period

9. 再實之木，其根必傷；多藏之家，其後必殃。

——《文子・符言》

1) If a tree bears fruit twice a year, its roots are damaged; if a household has too many treasures, its offspring will be in trouble.
2) If a tree bears fruit twice a year, its roots are damaged; if a household has collected too many treasures, its later generations will suffer.

—Wenzi, a Taoist work by unknown author of the Warring States Period

Terms:
a. 再實：一年結兩次果 to bear fruit twice a year
b. 後：後代 offspring

10. 智者舉事，因禍為福，轉敗為功。

——《史記・蘇秦列傳》

Wise people can turn misfortune to fortune and failure to success.

—Historical Records by Sima Qian (c.145 or 135 – ? BC) of the Han Dynasty

Terms:
舉事：處理事情 to deal with matters

（三）相對與絕對
Relative vs. Absolute

1. 一尺之棰，日取其半，萬世不竭。　　——《莊子‧天下》

If you keep cutting a foot-long stick by half daily,
you cannot finish the cutting in ten thousand years.

—Zhuangzi by Zhuang Zhou (c.369 – 286 BC)
and his followers of the Warring States Period

Terms:
a. 棰：棍棒 a stick
b. 竭：盡 to finish

2. 尺有所短，寸有所長。　　——戰國‧楚‧屈原《卜居》

A foot is short when compared with things longer; an
inch is long when compared with things shorter.

—Qu Yuan (c.340 – 277 BC), minister and poet
of the State of Chu of the Warring States Period

Comment: Relatively, everything in the world has its strength
and weakness.

3. 嶢嶢者易缺，皦皦者易污。　　——《後漢書‧黃瓊列傳》

1) Tall things easily get broken, and white things
easily get stained.
2) Tall things tend to get broken, and white things
tend to get stained.

—History of Eastern Han by Fan Ye (398 – 445), historian
of the State of Song of the Southern Dynasties

Terms:
a. 嶢嶢 (yáo)：高 tall
b. 皦皦 (jiǎo)：潔白 white

4. 枳句來巢，空穴來風。　　——戰國‧楚‧宋玉《風賦》

Because trifoliate orange trees have curving branches, birds come to nest in them; because caves are hollow, winds often blow into them.

—Song Yu, poet of the State of Chu
of the Warring States Period

Terms:

a. 枳 (zhǐ)：枸橘樹 trifoliate orange trees
b. 句 (gōu)：通 "勾"，彎曲 curving

Comment: There is a cause for what happens.

5. 珍其貨而後市，修其身而後交，善其謀而後動，成道也。　　—— 漢‧揚雄《法言‧修身》

Pack your goods and make them look good before selling them, cultivate your mind and integrity before you begin to make friends, try to make your strategy sound before taking action, and that is the way to succeed.

—Yang Xiong (53 BC – 18 AD), writer and
philosopher of the Western Han Dynasty

Terms:

a. 珍其貨：把貨物包裝得漂漂亮亮 to pack your goods and make them look good
b. 市：出售 to sell; to take to the market
c. 修其身：修養自身 to cultivate integrity
d. 交：交友 to make friends
e. 成道：成功之道 the way to succeed

6. 一條之枯，不損繁林之蓊藹。　　　——《抱朴子‧博喻》

A withered branch does not affect the exuberance of a forest.

—Baopuzi by Ge Hong (284–364) of the East Jin Dynasty

Terms:
a. 條：枝條 branches
b. 蓊藹 (wěng ǎi)：繁茂 exuberant

7. 名實相持而成，形影相應而立。　　——《韓非子‧功名》

The success of an official career interacts with external circumstances, the way a shadow does with the form of an object.

—Hanfeizi by Han Fei (c.280 – 233 BC), legalist
and statesman of late Warring States Period

Terms:
a. 名：功業 the success of an official career
b. 實：客觀實際 external circumstances; concrete reality
c. 相持：相互作用 to interact; to depend on
d. 相應：相依賴 to rely on each other

8. 一馬之奔，無一毛而不動；一舟之覆，
無一物而不沈。　　　—— 北周‧庾信《擬連珠》

When a horse gallops, every hair on his body moves with him; when a boat capsizes, everything on it sinks with it.

—Yu Xin (513 – 581), writer of the Northern Zhou Dynasty

Comment: Part goes with the whole.

9.　曾經滄海難為水，除卻巫山不是雲。

——唐·元稹《離思》

To those who have been to the ocean, the water elsewhere can hardly be called water; compared with Mt. Wu, the clouds elsewhere can hardly be called clouds.

—*Yuan Zhen (779 – 831), poet of the Tang Dynasty*

Terms:
a.　滄海：大海 sea; ocean
b.　巫山：山名，位於四川湖北交界處 a mountain lying between Sichuan and Hubei Provinces

Comment: He who has experienced or dealt with significant business is not bothered with insignificant things.

10.　毛羽未成，不可以高蜚。　　——《史記·蘇秦列傳》

If a bird is not full-fledged, it mustn't try to fly too high.

—*Historical Records by Sima Qian (c. 145 or 135 – ? BC) of the Han Dynasty*

Terms:
蜚 (fēi)：通"飛" to fly

11.　人在威，不在眾；……器在利，不在大。

—— 唐·白居易《漢高皇帝親斬白蛇賦》

Man's power lies in fortitude, not in multitude; …the function of a tool lies in its sharpness, not in its size.

—*Bai Juyi (772 – 846), poet of the Tang Dynasty*

12. 非知之艱，行之惟艱。　　　　　——《尚書‧説命中》

1) It is not difficult to understand, but it is difficult to practise.
2) The difficult thing is not understanding, but practice.

—Collection of Ancient Texts, a Confucian classic

13. 好事盡從難處得，少年無向易中輕。

——唐‧李咸用《送譚孝廉赴舉》

All good things are achieved through difficulties and hardships, so young people must not take things easy and expect to attain anything effortlessly.

—Li Xianyong of the Tang Dynasty

Terms:

a. 盡：都 all
b. 少年：年輕人 young people
c. 易：容易的事情 easy things
d. 輕：輕取 to attain without effort

14. 事者，難成而易敗也；名者，難立而易廢也。

——《淮南子‧人間訓》

Things are difficult to succeed but easy to fail; reputations are difficult to establish but easy to ruin.

—Huainanzi by Prince of Huainan Liu An (179 – 122 BC)
and some of his followers of the Western Han Dynasty

（四）實踐出真知
True Knowledge Comes from Practice

1.   百聞不如一見。   ——《漢書·趙充國傳》

To hear one hundred times is not as reliable as to see only once.

—History of Han, chronicle of the Han Dynasty
between 206 BC and 23 AD, by Ban Gu (32 – 92)

2.   讀書雖可喜，何如躬踐履。   ——清·劉岩《雜詩》

Reading is a delightful thing, but it is incomparable with personal practice.

—Liu Yan (1656 –1716) of the Qing Dynasty

Terms:
a. 躬：親自；親身 personal; by oneself
b. 踐履：實踐 to practice; practice

（五）權衡
Weigh and Measure

1.   權，然後知輕重；度，然後知長短。

——《孟子·梁惠王上》

Weigh it on the scale and you know its weight; measure it with a ruler and you know its length.

—Mencius by Meng Ke (c.372 – 289 BC), philosopher
and Confucian scholar of the Warring States Period

Terms:

a. 權：用秤稱 to weigh on the scale

b. 度（duó）：用尺量 to measure with a ruler

2. 漁不竭澤，畋不合圍。

—— 唐・白居易《策林二・養動植之物》

1) Do not dry up the pond when you fish; do not round up the animals when you hunt.

2) Do not fish by drying up the pond, and do not hunt by rounding up the animals.

—Bai Juyi (772 – 846), poet of the Tang Dynasty

Terms:

a. 竭澤：把水抽乾 to dry up the pond / river

b. 畋（tián）：打獵 to hunt

3. 小不忍則亂大謀。   ——《論語・衛靈公》

1) Lack of self-restraint in small matters may ruin one's strategic plans.

2) Failing to practice self-restraint in small matters may spoil one's grave undertakings.

—The Analects, a Confucian classic recording the words and deeds of Confucius and his dialogues with his disciples

4. 成大事者不惜小費。   ——《金瓶梅》

People who are dedicated to a noble cause do not bother about trifling expenses.

—Plum in the Gold Vase, a novel first published in early 17th century

5. 識遠者貴本，見近者務末。 ——《抱朴子·博喻》

1) Far-sighted people cherish the roots and trunk of the tree, while near-sighted people go for the tip of it.

2) Far-sighted people cherish the important aspects of things, while near-sighted people go for the minor details.

—*Baopuzi by Ge Hong (284 – 364) of the East Jin Dynasty*

Terms:

a. 貴：以⋯⋯為貴 to cherish; to think of something as important

b. 務：追求 to go for

6. 逐鹿者不顧兔，決千金之貨者不爭銖兩之價。

——《淮南子·説林訓》

A hunter after a deer is not distracted by a hare, and a man doing business of ten thousand pieces of gold does not haggle over the weight of one or two grams.

—*Huainanzi by the Prince of Huainan Liu An (179 – 122 BC) and some of his followers of the Western Han Dynasty*

Terms:

a. 銖（zhū）兩：很小的重量單位，意指 "很小" a small unit of weight

b. 不顧：不注意 not distracted

c. 不爭：不計較 not to haggle over

7. 枉尺而直尋，宜若可為也。 ——《孟子·滕文公下》

By bending one foot you can make eight feet straight. This is something worth the effort.

—*Mencius by Meng Ke (c.372 – 289 BC), philosopher and Confucian scholar of the Warring States Period*

Terms:
a. 枉：使彎曲 to bend
b. 直：使伸直 to straighten
c. 尋：古代長度單位，約合八尺 unit of length in ancient China, roughly equal to eight feet

8. 人無遠慮，必有近憂。 ——《論語 • 衛靈公》

If one does not take a long view of things, he will be plagued by imminent worries.

—The Analects, a Confucian classic recording
the words and deeds of Confucius and his dialogues with his disciples

9. 審毫厘之計者，必遺天下之大數。

——《淮南子 • 主術訓》

If one is over-calculating in trivialities, he is sure to fail in momentous strategies of national importance.

—Huainanzi by the Prince of Huainan Liuan(179 – 122BC)
and some of his followers of the Western Han Dynasty

Terms:
a. 審：考慮 to be calculating
b. 大數：大的謀略 momentous strategies

（六）道不可言，真理不滅
Tao and Truth

1.　道可道，非常道；名可名，非常名。

——《老子・道經一》

The Tao that can be described is not the eternal Tao;
the Name that can be named is not the eternal name.

—Laozi by Li Er (李耳), philosopher of late Spring
and Autumn Period, and founder of Taoism

Terms:
a. 道：第一個"道"指道家所説的"道"Tao
　　第二個"道"指"描述"to describe
b. 常道：永恆的道 the eternal Tao
c. 名：第一個"名"指"道"的所稱 Name of Tao
　　第二個"名"是"説出"的意思 to name

2.　大道不稱，大辯不言。　　——《莊子・齊物論》

The great Tao cannot be enunciated, and great
eloquence does not resort to words.

—Zhuangzi by Zhuang Zhou (c.369 – 286 BC)
and his followers of the Warring States Period

Terms:
不稱：説不出 cannot be enunciated

3.　至則不論，論則不至。　　——《莊子・知北遊》

If one has reached the realm of Tao, he does not talk
about it; if he talks about Tao, he has not reached the
realm of it.

—Zhuangzi by Zhuang Zhou (c.369 – 286 BC)
and his followers of the Warring States Period

Terms:

a. 至：達到 "道" 的境界 to reach the realm of Tao

b. 論：談論（"道"）to talk (about Tao)

4.　國有亡主而世無廢道。　　　　　——《淮南子‧主術訓》

1) There might be a toppled monarch in a country, but there is never invalidated truth in the world.

2) The monarch of a country can be toppled, but truth can never be invalidated.

—Huainanzi by the Prince of Huainan Liu An (179 – 122 BC)
and some of his followers of the Western Han Dynasty

Terms:

a. 亡主：被推翻的君主 toppled monarch

b. 道：指真理 truth

5.　往者雖舊，餘味日新。

　　　　　—— 南朝‧梁‧劉勰《文心雕龍‧宗經》

Although previous classics were written in the past, their significance and implications are renewed daily.

— The Literary Mind and the Carving of the Dragon
by Liu Xie (c.465 – 532) of the State of Liang of the Southern Dynasties

Terms:

往者：指前代經書 previous classics

6.　積微，月不勝日，時不勝月，歲不勝時。

　　　　　——《荀子‧強國》

In terms of accumulating, it is better to do it by the day than by the month, better by the month than by the season, better by the season than by the year.

—Xunzi by Xun Kuang (313 – 238 BC), thinker
and educator of the Warring States Period

Terms:

不勝：不如 not as good as

7.　**高以下基，洪由纖起。**　　——晉・張華《勵志詩》九首其八

Height is built on low foundations, and greatness grows out of what is small.

—Zhang Hua (232 – 300) of the Jin Dynasty

Terms:
a. 下：低矮的東西 low things
b. 基：基礎 foundation
c. 洪：宏大 greatness
d. 纖：細小的東西 small things

8.　**山不讓塵，川不辭盈。**　　——晉・張華《勵志詩》九首其七

1) Mountains do not reject fine dust, and rivers do not refuse to fill with water.
2) Mountains are high because they do not reject fine dust; rivers are deep because they do not refuse to fill with water.

—Zhang Hua (232 – 300) of the Jin Dynasty

Terms:
a. 讓：捨棄 to reject
b. 辭：拒絕 to refuse
c. 盈：滿 fullness

9.　**千里始足下，高山起微塵。**　　——《老子・德經六十四》

A thousand-*li* journey begins with the first step, and a high mountain is built up with fine dust.

—Laozi by Li Er (李耳 *), philosopher of late Spring and Autumn Period, and founder of Taoism*

10. 事有緣微而成著，物有治近而致遠。

——《抱朴子‧廣譬》

1) There are instances in which notable accomplishments are achieved through commitment to insignificant things, and long-term objectives realized through current undertakings.

2) There are people who achieve notable accomplishments by committing to insignificant things, and people who realize long-term objectives (or reap long-term benefit) by devoting themselves to current undertakings.

—Baopuzi by Ge Hong (284 – 364) of the East Jin Dynasty

Terms:

a. 緣：因為；通過 because of; through

b. 緣微：因為小事；通過小事情 because of small things; through small things

c. 治近：做眼前的事情 current undertaking

d. 致遠：實現長遠的目標；得到長遠好處 to realize long-term objectives; to reap long-term benefit

11. 積德累行，不知其善，有時而用；
棄義背理，不知其惡，有時而亡。

——《漢書‧枚乘傳》

1) When you keep cultivating your virtue and doing kind things, though you are unaware what is the good it does, the effect will make itself felt in time; when you reject righteous principles and violate conventions, though you are unaware what is the evil it does, you will find yourself ruined by it when the time comes.

2) When you keep cultivating your virtue and doing kind things, you may not know what is the good

in it, but the effect will make itself felt in time;
when you reject righteous principles and violate
conventions, you may not know what is the evil in
it, but you will find yourself ruined by it when the
time comes.

—History of Han, chronicle of the Han Dynasty
between 206 BC and 23 AD by Ban Gu (32 – 92)

Terms:

a. 不知其善：不知道有甚麼好處 unaware of the good it does
b. 有時：到時候 in time
c. 不知其惡：不知道有甚麼壞處 unaware of the evil it does

12. 不知溪水長，只覺釣船高。　　——明・偰遜《山雨》

Without awareness of the water rising, I only feel the
boat coming up.

— "Mountain Rain" by Xie Xun of the Ming Dynasty

Terms:

長（zhǎng）：上升 to rise

Note:

These two lines were commended as "nature-inspired" by Shen
Deqian (1673 – 1769), poet of the Qing Dynasty.

13. 為者常成，行者常至。　　——《晏子春秋・內篇・雜下》

He who keeps working will achieve his goal; he who
keeps walking will arrive at his destination.

—Yanzi's Spring and Autumn Annals, supposedly written
by Yan Ying (? – 500 BC), minister of the State of Qi
during the Spring and Autumn Period

14. 臨河羨魚，不如歸家織網。　　──《淮南子‧說林訓》

1) It's no use standing by the river and admiring others fishing; It's better to go back home and knit your own net instead.

2) Go back home and knit your own net instead of standing by the river and admiring others fishing.

—Huainanzi by Prince Huainan Liu An (179 – 122 BC) and some of his followers of the Western Han Dynasty

Terms:

羨魚：羨慕別人捕魚 to admire others fishing

15. 不入虎穴，焉得虎子。　　──《後漢書‧班超列傳》

If you don't enter the lair, how can you capture the tiger's cubs?

—History of Eastern Han by Fan Ye (398 – 445), historian of the State of Song of the Southern Dynasties

Terms:

焉：怎麼能夠 How can you...

Comment: If one intends to be successful in life, he has to undergo hardships and take risks sometimes.

16. 雖有天下易生之物也，一日暴之，十日寒之，
未有能生者也。　　──《孟子‧告子上》

Although there are crops that you can raise most easily, if you leave them exposed to the sun for one day and then leave them open to the cold for ten days, they cannot grow well.

—Mencius by Meng Ke (c.372 – 289 BC), philosopher and Confucian scholar of the Warring States Period

Terms:
a. 暴（pù）：曝；曬 to expose to the sun
b. 寒：使寒冷 to make...cold

（七）善始善終
Begin Well and End Well

1. 善始者實繁，克終者蓋寡。 ——唐·魏徵《諫太宗十思疏》

1) Many people can begin well, but not many of them can end well.
2) There are many people who can do well at the beginning, but few can keep doing well till the end.

—Wei Zheng (580 – 643), statesman of the Tang Dynasty

Terms:
a. 繁：多 many
b. 寡：少 few
c. 克：能 to be able to
d. 蓋：大概 probably

2. 慎終如始，則無敗事。 ——《老子·德經六十四》

1) If you exercise as much prudence at the end as at the beginning, there is no chance of failure.
2) If you conduct your undertaking carefully throughout, you can never fail.

—Laozi by Li Er (李耳), philosopher of late Spring and Autumn Period, and founder of Taoism

3. 行百里者半於九十，此言末路之難。

——《戰國策·秦策》

Ninety *li* out of a hundred-*li* journey is only half way through, which means the going becomes tougher toward the end.

—*Strategies of the Warring States compiled by Liu Xiang*
(c.77 – 6 BC) of the Western Han Dynasty

Terms:

半：等於一半 half way through

4. 升峻者患於垂上而力不足。　　——《抱朴子·極言》

What a climber worries about is that when he gets close to the top, his strength falters.

—*Baopuzi by Ge Hong (284 – 364) of the East Jin Dynasty*

Terms:

a. 峻 (jùn)：高 high
b. 患：擔心 to worry
c. 垂：將近 near

（八）果斷成事，猶豫無功
Be Decisive

1. 斷而敢行，鬼神避之。　　——《史記·李斯列傳》

1) Courage and decisiveness keep ghosts away.
2) When you are decisive and have the courage to act, even ghosts will stay away.

—*Historical Records by Sima Qian (c.145*
or 135 – ? BC) of the Han Dynasty

2.　狐欲渡河，無奈尾何。　　　——清‧沈德潛《古詩源》

When a fox is going to cross the river, he worries about his tail getting wet.

> —*Origin of Ancient Poetry compiled by Shen Deqian (1673 – 1769), poet of the Qing Dynasty*

Note:

The fox cherishes his tail very much. When it begins to cross a river, it holds its tail above water; but when it gets midstream and tired, its tail may drop into the water. Metaphorically, sometimes indecisiveness out of apprehension can spoil things.

3.　智者不再計，勇士不怯死。　——《史記‧魯仲連鄒陽列傳》

A wise man does not hesitate, and a brave man is not afraid of death.

> —*Historical Records by Sima Qian (c.145 or 135 – ? BC) of the Han Dynasty*

Terms:

a. 再計：三心二意 to hesitate
b. 怯：怕 be afraid of

4.　失火之家，豈暇先言大人而後救火乎？

　　　　　　　　　　——《史記‧齊悼惠王世家》

When your house is on fire, do you have time to inform your elders first and then put it out?

> —*Historical Records by Sima Qian (c.145 or 135 – ? BC) of the Han Dynasty*

Terms:

a. 暇：來得及 to have time to
b. 言：稟告 to tell; to inform

（九）功以謀就
Think before You Act

1. 君子計成而後行。　　　　　——《國語·魯語下》

1) Think before you act.
2) Planning goes before acting.
3) An honourable man always thinks carefully before
   acting.

—Remarks of Monarchs, history of late Western Zhou Dynasty
and other major states in the Spring and Autumn Period,
attributed to Zuo Qiuming, historian of the State of Lu

2. 計勝怒則強，怒勝計則亡。　　——《荀子·哀公》

If your strategic resources overcome anger, you
are strong; if your anger overcomes your strategic
resources, you will perish.

—Xunzi by Xun Kuang (313 – 238 BC), thinker
and educator of the Warring States Period

3. 事以密成，語以泄敗。　　　　——《韓非子·説難》

If you can keep secret, you succeed; if the secret is let
out by word of mouth, you fail.

—Hanfeizi by Han Fei (c.280 – 233 BC), legalist
and statesman of late Warring States Period

4. 聲無細而不聞，行無隱而不形。　——《慎子·外篇》

No sound is inaudible, however slight it is; no conduct
is imperceptible, however private it is.

—Shenzi by Shen Dao of the Warring States Period

Terms:

無：無論 no matter how

（十）舉綱張目
Take the Key

1. **善張網者引其綱。**　　　——《韓非子‧外儲説右下》

A good fisherman casts his fishing net by the control rope.

—Hanfeizi by Han Fei (c.280 – 233 BC), legalist
and statesman of late Warring States Period

Terms:
a. 引：拉 to pull
b. 綱：網的總繩 control rope

2. **以簡制煩惑，以易御險難。**　　——《尹文子‧大道上》

Solve complex and perplexing problems by simple means, and handle dangerous and difficult problems in easy ways.

—YinWenzi by Yin Wen of the Warring States Period

Terms:
a. 制：解決 to solve
b. 御：駕馭 to handle; to overcome

3. **執一而應萬，握要而治詳。**　　——《淮南子‧人間訓》

Grasp the key and you can deal with many problems; take the key and you can cope with trivial details.

—Huainanzi by the Prince of Huainan Liu An (179 – 122 BC)
and some of his followers of the Western Han Dynasty

Terms:
a. 執：掌握 to grasp
b. 一：關鍵 the key
c. 應：應對 to deal with
d. 要：關鍵 the key
e. 詳：細節 details

4. 挽弓當挽強，用箭當用長。
射人先射馬，擒賊先擒王。

—— 唐・杜甫《前出塞》九首之六

Choose a tight bow to bend,
Choose a long arrow to shoot.
To shoot the horseman, shoot the horse first,
To capture the bandits, capture their chieftain first.

—Du Fu (712 – 770), poet of the Tang Dynasty

Terms:
a. 挽：拉 to bend a bow
b. 強：有力的 tight; tough

（十一） 由表及裏，由此及彼
From the Exterior to the Interior, from One to the Other

1. 國家將興，必有禎祥；國家將亡，必有妖孽。

——《禮記・中庸》

When the country is going to thrive, there must be good omens for it; when the country is going to fall, there must be abnormalities for it.

—The Book of Rites, a Confucian classic

Terms:
a. 禎（zhēn）祥：吉祥之兆 good omens; auspicious signs
b. 妖孽：古代指物類反常現象 abnormalities

2.　見一葉落而知歲之將暮。　　　　──《淮南子・説山訓》

1) A fallen leaf tells that the year is nearing its end.
2) A fallen leaf predicts the end of the year.

—Huainanzi by the Prince of Huainan Liu An (179 – 122 BC)
and some of his followers of the Western Han Dynasty

Terms:
a. 歲：年 year
b. 暮：年終 end of the year

3.　漁者走淵，木者走山。　　　　──《淮南子・説林訓》

Fishermen go to the water, and lumbermen go to the mountain.

—Huainanzi by the Prince of Huainan Liu An (179 – 122 BC)
and some of his followers of the Western Han Dynasty

Terms:
a. 漁者：打魚的人 fisherman
b. 木者：伐木的人 lumberman
c. 走：走向 to go toward
d. 淵：水邊 water

4.　見象牙乃知其大於牛，見虎尾乃知其大於狸。

──《淮南子・説林訓》

1) When you see an elephant's tusk, you know it is larger than a cow; when you see a tiger's tail, you know it is larger than a wildcat.

2) An elephant's tusk tells that an elephant is bigger than a cow; a tiger's tail tells that a tiger is bigger than a wildcat.

—Huainanzi by Prince Huainan Liu An (179 – 122 BC) and some of his followers of the Western Han Dynasty

Terms:

狸：野貓 wildcat

5. 睹木不瘁，則悟美玉之在山；覿岸不枯，則覺明珠之沈淵。　　──《抱朴子·清鑒》

1) When you see luxuriant trees, you should know there is beautiful jade in the mountain; when you see exuberant grass on the banks, you should know there are precious pearls deep in the water.

2) Luxuriant trees tell there is beautiful jade in the mountain; exuberant grass on the banks tells there are precious pearls deep in the water.

—Baopuzi by Ge Hong (284 – 364) of the East Jin Dynasty

Terms:

a. 瘁（cuì）：凋敝 to wilt; to wither

b. 覿（dí）：看見 to see

Comment: This quote tells that one should try to see the interior through the exterior. It also tells that in prosperous places you can always find outstanding people.

十四、治國
Govern the Country

（一）民
The People

1. 國以民為基，貴以賤為本。　——《王符·潛夫論·救邊》

　　1) A country takes its people as its foundation; the noble takes the humble as their base.

　　2) The people are the foundation of a country; the humble are the base of the noble.

—Social Evils through the Eye of a Hermit by Wang Fu
(c.85 – 162), philosopher of the Eastern Han Dynasty

2. 近者說，遠者來。　——《論語·子路》

　　1) Make those near you happy, and attract those far away from you to come.

　　2) Make those near you happy to be your citizens, and make those abroad willing to come to live and work under you.

—The Analects, a Confucian classic recording
the words and deeds of Confucius and
his dialogues with his disciples

Terms:

說：通 "悅" (yuè) to be happy

3. 善御者不忘其馬，善射者不忘其弩。

————《淮南子‧繆稱訓》

A good carriage driver does not ignore his horses, and
a good archer does not ignore his bows.

—*Huainanzi by Prince Huainan Liu An (179 – 122 BC)*
and some of his followers of the Western Han Dynasty

Terms:
a. 御：駕車 to guide a carriage
b. 弩：弓 bows

4. 民之所欲，天必從之。   ————《尚書‧泰誓上》

Heaven will obey what people desire.

—*Collection of Ancient Texts, a Confucian classic*

5. 字人無異術，至論不如清。 ——唐‧杜荀鶴《送人宰吳縣》

There is no special method for loving the people. In
the final analysis, the best way to do it is to be clean
and honest.

—*Du Xunhe of the Tang Dynasty*

Terms:
a. 字人：愛人民 to love the people
b. 至論：說到底 in the final analysis
c. 清：廉明正直 clean and honest

6. 安得壯士挽天河，淨洗甲兵長不用。

————唐‧杜甫《洗兵馬》

How I wish I could get some warrior to pour the water
from the Heavenly River (the Milky Way) and wash
the armors and arms off the earth for good.

—*Du Fu (712 – 770), poet of the Tang Dynasty*

Terms:

a. 天河：銀河 the Heavenly River; the Milky Way
b. 甲兵：鎧甲和兵器 armors and arms

7. 誰知盤中餐，粒粒皆辛苦。　　——唐・李紳《憫農》

A grain of rice in the bowl, a drop of sweat in the field.

—Li Shen, poet of the Tang Dynasty

8. 生無一日之歡，死有萬世之名。　——《列子・楊朱篇》

When alive, they never had the joy of life for a single day; when dead, they enjoyed posthumous fame for thousands of years to come.

—Liezi, a Taoist Classical work by Lie Yukou
of the Warring States Period

Note:

The two lines refer to the four ancient sages：Yao（堯）, Shun（舜）, Duke of Zhou（周公）and Confucius（孔子）.

9. 先天下之憂而憂，後天下之樂而樂。

——宋・范仲淹《嶽陽樓記》

When the people of the country have something to worry about, I am the first to worry about it; when the people of the country have something to enjoy, I am the last to enjoy it.

—Fan Zhongyan (989 – 1052),
scholar of the Northern Song Dynasty

10. 民可百年無貨，不可一朝有飢。

——北朝・北魏・賈思勰《齊民要術》

The people can do without jewels and treasures for

a hundred years, but they must not go hungry for a single day.

—Important Arts for the People's Welfare by Jia Sixie,
agronomist of the Northern Wei Dynasty (386 – 534)

Terms:
貨：金銀財寶 jewels and treasures

11. 得人者興，失人者崩。　　　　——《史記・商君列傳》

He who wins the heart of the people thrives; he who loses the heart of the people perishes.

—Historical Records by Sima Qian (c.145
or 135 – ? BC) of the Han Dynasty

Terms:
人：人心 the heart of the people

12. 敬賢如大賓，愛民如赤子。　—— 漢・路溫舒《尚德緩刑書》

Respect the virtuous and capable people like distinguished guests, and love the ordinary people like newborns.

—Lu Wenshu of the Han Dynasty

Terms:
a. 大賓：尊貴的客人 distinguished guests
b. 赤子：初生嬰兒 newborn babies; innocent children

13. 魚失水則死，水失魚猶為水也。　　　——《尸子》

Fish taken out of water will die, but water without fish is still water.

—Shizi by Shi Jiao (c.390 – 330), thinker
and statesman of the Warring States Period

（二）居安思危，謹慎為政
Think of Peril in Peace and Exercise Prudence in Politics

1. 興必慮衰，安必思危。　　　——《史記・司馬相如列傳》

When the country is rising, one must think of the possibility of its falling; when the country is stable and peaceful, one must be prepared for possible turbulences.

—Historical Records by Sima Qian (c.145 or 135 – ?BC) of the Han Dynasty

Terms:
a. 興：興盛 to thrive
b. 慮：想到 to think of

2. 國雖大，好戰必亡；天下雖平，忘戰必危。

——《史記・平津侯主父列傳》

A warlike country, however powerful, is sure to fall; a stable and peaceful country, if unaware of the threat of war, will be in danger.

—Historical Records by Sima Qian (c.145 or 135 – ? BC) of the Han Dynasty

3. 水則載舟，水則覆舟。　　　——《荀子・王制》

Water can float a boat, and it can also capsize it.

—Xunzi by Xun Kuang (313 – 238 BC), thinker and educator of the Warring States Period

Terms:
a. 則：也 also

b. 載：托浮 to float
c. 覆：使……傾覆 to capsize

4. 政有毫髮之善，下必知也。

—— 唐·白居易《策林四·采詩》

1) The slightest good politics does can be felt by the people.
2) The people can feel the advantage politics brings about, however slight it is.

—Bai Juyi (772 – 846), poet of the Tang Dynasty

Terms:
a. 政：政治 politics
b. 毫髮之善：一點點好處 the slightest good
c. 下：下層百姓 the people

（三）為政有術
Art of Government

1. 為善不同，同歸於治；為惡不同，同歸於亂。

——《尚書·蔡仲之命》

Although there are different ways to practice benevolent government, they all lead to peace and stability; although there are different ways to exercise tyrannical rule, they all lead to disorder and upheaval.

—Collection of Ancient Texts, a Confucian classic

Terms:
a. 為善：實行善政 to practise benevolent government
b. 治：社會安定 social stability

2. 徒善不足以為政，徒法不能以自行。

——《孟子·離婁上》

Benevolence alone is not enough for the governing of the country; laws alone cannot be enforced by themselves.

— Mencius by Meng Ke (c.372 – 289 BC), philosopher
and Confucian scholar of the Warring States Period

Terms:

徒：僅僅 alone; only

3. 因其性則天下聽從，拂其性則法縣而不用。

——《淮南子·泰族訓》

If what you do is in conformity with human nature, the people will obey you; if what you do violates human nature, the people will not be dictated to even if corporal punishment is enforced.

— Huainanzi by Prince Huainan Liu An (179 – 122 BC)
and some of his followers of the Western Han Dynasty

Terms:

a. 因：順乎 in conformity with
b. 拂：違逆 to violate
c. 縣（xuán）：通 "懸" to apply corporal punishment

4. 罷無能，廢無用，損不急之官，塞私門之請。

——《戰國策·秦策》

Dismiss the incompetent, exterminate the useless, cut down the unnecessary, and stop backdoorism.

— Strategies of the Warring States compiled by Liu Xiang
(c.77 – 6 BC) of the Western Han Dynasty

Terms:

a. 罷：解除 to dismiss
b. 廢：廢除 to exterminate
c. 損：減少 to cut down
d. 塞：堵塞 to stop

（四）鑒古知今
Learn from History

1. 明鏡者，所以察形也；往古者，所以知今也。

——《大戴禮記·保傳》

Mirror is used to reflect how you look; ancient history
is studied to infer what will happen today.

—Da Dai's Book of Rites compiled by Dai De,
scholar on rites of the Western Han Dynasty

Terms:

往古者：古代歷史 ancient history

2. 前事之不忘，後事之師。　　　　——《戰國策·趙策》

Remember what happened in the past as a lesson for
the future.

—Strategies of the Warring States compiled by Liu Xiang
(c.77 – 6 BC) of the Western Han Dynasty

（五）忠於職守
Do Your Best to Carry out Your Duties

1. 居之無倦，行之以忠。　　　　　　——《論語・顏淵》

Do not slack off on your duties and execute orders to the letter.

—The Analects, a Confucian classic recording
the words and deeds of Confucius and his dialogues with his disciples

Terms:
a. 居之：擔任職務 to take official duties
b. 行之：執行命令 to carry out orders

2. 鞠躬盡瘁，死而後已。　　——三國・諸葛亮《後出師表》

I'll exercise the utmost care and spare no effort in performing my duties.

—Zhuge Liang (181 – 234), statesman and strategist
of the State of Shu of the Three Kingdoms

Terms:
a. 鞠躬：彎腰，這裏引申為恭敬謹慎 to bend one's back; to exercise respect and care
b. 盡瘁（cuì）：盡己所能 to spare no effort in performing one's duties

3. 春蠶到死絲方盡，蠟炬成灰淚始乾。

——唐・李商隱《無題》

A spring silkworm won't stop spinning silk until it dies; a candle won't stop shedding tears until it burns up (or becomes ashes).

—Li Shangyin (c.812 or 813 – c.858),
poet of the Tang Dynasty

4. 居官者當事不避難。　　　　　——《國語・魯語上》

An official should not evade difficulties he is confronted with.

*—Remarks of Monarchs, history of late Western Zhou Dynasty
and other major states in the Spring and Autumn Period,
attributed to Zuo Qiuming, historian of the State of Lu*

5. 極身無貳慮，盡公而不顧私。　——《史記・范睢蔡澤列傳》

Do your best with complete devotion, and apply yourself to the public interest without consideration for yourself.

*—Historical Records by Sima Qian (c.145
or 135 – ? BC) of the Han Dynasty*

Terms:
a. 極身：盡自身之所能 to do your best
b. 無貳慮：沒有二心 with complete devotion

6. 敬其事而後其食。　　　　　　——《論語・衛靈公》

1) Render a good service first and then take the payment.
2) Perform your duties well and then take the reward.

*—The Analects, a Confucian classic recording the words and
deeds of Confucius and his dialogues with his disciples*

Terms:
a. 敬：認真對待；認真做 to render a good service
b. 食：領取俸祿 to take the payment

7. 官非其任不處也，祿非其功不受也。

——《史記・日者列傳》

1) Do not take the appointment you are not supposed to; do not accept the payment you do not deserve.
2) Do not take the assignment you are not supposed to; do not accept the reward if you have not done the service to deserve it.

—Historical Records by Sima Qian (c.145 or 135 – ? BC) of the Han Dynasty

Terms:

a. 任：所擔任的職務 position assigned to
b. 不處（chǔ）：不在其位 not to take
c. 祿：俸祿；報酬 payment; reward
d. 功：功勞 services rendered

8. 人當使器之有餘於受，無使受之有餘於器。

——明・莊元臣《叔苴子》

One should have greater capabilities than the position and the reward offered, not vice versa.

—Zhuang Yuanchen (1560 – 1609) of the Ming Dynasty

Terms:

a. 器：才能 capability
b. 受：所受的職位和報酬 the position and the reward offered
c. 無：不 not

十五、文學藝術
Literature and Art

（一）文與行
Writing and Conduct

1. 心之孔嘉，其言藹如。 ——清・袁枚《續詩品・齊心》

An angelic nature / temperament makes one's words gentle and affable.

—Yuan Mei (1716 – 1798), poet of the Qing Dynasty

Terms:
a. 孔嘉：甚好；甚美 good; beautiful; angelic
b. 藹如：和氣的樣子 gentle and affable

2. 文以行立，行以文傳。

——南朝・梁・劉勰《文心雕龍・宗經》

The excellence of writing depends on moral integrity, and moral integrity is reflected in writing.

—The Literary Mind and the Carving of the Dragon by Liu Xie (c.465 – 532) of the State of Liang of the Southern Dynasties

Terms:
a. 文：文章 writing
b. 傳：表現 to reflect; to represent

3. 凡作人貴直，而作詩文貴曲。　——清‧袁枚《隨園詩話》

1) The best policy in conducting oneself is to be straightforward, but the best policy in writing is to be inflectional.

2) The best way to conduct oneself is to be straightforward, but the best way to write is to be curving.

—Yuan Mei (1716 – 1798), poet of the Qing Dynasty

4. 有佳意必有佳語。　——清‧孫聯奎《詩品臆說》

1) Good conception gives rise to good expression.

2) Good expression comes from good conception.

3) Well-conceived, well expressed.

—Sun Liankui of the Qing Dynasty

5. 狀難寫之景如在目前，含不盡之意見於言外。

—— 宋‧歐陽修《六一詩話》引梅堯臣

Describe the scenes that are difficult to describe as vividly as if it is right before your eyes, and imply the profound meaning between the lines.

—quoted from Mei Yaochen, poet of the Northern Song Dynasty, by Ouyang Xiu (1007 – 1072)

Terms:

狀：描寫 to portray；to describe

6. 因字而生句，積句而成章，積章而成篇。

—— 南朝‧梁‧劉勰《文心雕龍‧章句》

1) Individual words make a sentence, sentences make a section, and sections make a discourse.

2) A discourse is made up of sections, a section is made up of sentences, and a sentence is made up of individual words.

—The Literary Mind and the Carving of the Dragon by Liu Xie
(c.465 – 532) of the State of Liang of the Southern Dynasties

7. 寫神則生，寫貌則死。 ——清・許槤《六朝文絜》

Capture the inner spirit, and you can make the writing vivid; confine yourself to the outer appearance, and your writing will be rigid.

—Xu Lian (1787 – 1862), scholar of the Qing Dynasty

Terms:
a. 神：精神 spirit
b. 貌：外貌 appearance
c. 生：生動 vivid
d. 死：死板 rigid

8. 不精不誠，不能動人。 ——《莊子・漁父》

Insincerity does not appeal to the heart.

—Zhuangzi by Zhuang Zhou (c.369 – 286 BC)
and his followers of the Warring States Period

9. 情以物興，物以情觀。

——南朝・梁・劉勰《文心雕龍・詮賦》

The author's feelings is evoked by external realities, and external realities are expressed through the author's feelings.

—The Literary Mind and the Carving of the Dragon
by Liu Xie (c.465 – 532) of the State of Liang of the Southern Dynasties

Terms:
a. 物：外物；客觀事物 external realities
b. 興：產生 to be evoked
c. 觀：表現 to be expressed

10. 修辭立其誠。　　　　　　　　——《周易・乾・文言》

Good writing is based on truth and trustworthiness.

—The Book of Changes, a Confucian classic

Terms:
a. 修辭：這裏指寫作文章 writings
b. 誠：真實可信 true and trustworthy

（二）風格
Style

1.　文變染乎世情，興廢繫乎時序。

　　　　　　　—— 南朝・梁・劉勰《文心雕龍・時序》

The change of writing style is influenced by the ways of the world, and the realm of literature rises and falls with the change of times.

—The Literary Mind and the Carving of the Dragon by
Liu Xie (c.465 – 532) of the State of Liang
of the Southern Dynasties

Terms:
a. 文變：文風的變化 the change of writing style
b. 染：影響 to influence; to affect
c. 興廢：興衰 to rise and fall
d. 時序：時代變遷 change of the times

2. 美人姿態在嫩，詩家姿態在老。

——清・賀貽孫《詩筏》

The charm of a beautiful woman lies in her tender and graceful bearing, but the beauty of a poet lies in his mature and seasoned manner of expression.

—He Yisun of the Qing Dynasty

3. 文章易作，逋峭難為。　　　——清・袁枚《隨園詩話》

It is easy to write, but difficult to create a flavour in writing.

—Yuan Mei (1716 – 1798), poet of the Qing Dynasty

Terms:

逋峭 (bū qiào)：指文章有風致 to create a flavour in writing

4. 要辭達而理舉，故無取乎冗長。　　——晉・陸機《文賦》

The important thing in writing is to be expressive and make your point clear; lengthiness is not advisable.

—Wenfu, a theoretic work on literary writing,
written in the form of rhyme prose, by Lu Ji (261 – 303),
writer of the Western Jin Dynasty (265 – 317)

Terms:

a. 辭達：文辭能表達思想 to be expressive
b. 理舉：把道理講清楚 to make the point clear
c. 冗長：文章不簡練 lengthy

5. 言有盡而意無窮者，天下之至言也。

—— 宋‧姜夔《白石道人詩說》引蘇軾

Words with lingering flavours are the best.

—quoted from Su Shi, poet of the Northern Song Dynasty,
by Jiang Kui, scholar of the Southern Song Dynasty

Terms:

無窮：無盡 with a flavour lingering on

6. 詩畫本一律，天工與清新。

—— 宋‧蘇軾《書鄢陵王主簿所畫折枝二首》其一

Poetry and painting meet the same aesthetic requirements: superb artistic skill and fresh lucid style.

—Su Shi (1037 – 1101), alias Su Dongpo,
poet of the Northern Song Dynasty

7. 景是眾人同，情乃一人領。 —— 清‧袁枚《人老莫作詩》

The scene appears the same to everybody, but it is felt differently by each individual.

—Yuan Mei (1716 – 1798), poet of the Qing Dynasty

8. 不著一字，盡得風流。 —— 唐‧司空圖《詩品‧含蓄》

Though not a single word is literally applied to the subject, the literary aesthetic gracefulness is fully represented.

—Sikong Tu (837 – 908), poet of the Tang Dynasty

Terms:

a. 著（zhuó）：寫上 to write
b. 風流：指文學作品的超逸美妙 literary aesthetic gracefulness

Stroke Index
筆畫索引

This index is arranged by stroke count (the number of strokes) in the first character.

1 畫 stroke

一尺之棰，… 179
一年之計，… 84
一言僨事，… 91
一晝一夜，… 174
一馬之奔，… 181
一能之士，… 99
一條之枯，… 181
一叢深色花，… 117

2 畫 strokes

人一能之，… 158
人之患，… 16
人不可以無恥，… 30
人必有才也而後能憐才，… 85
人生天地之間，… 170
人生何謂富？ 49
人在威，… 182
人有盜而富者，… 107
人固不易知，… 69
人固有一死，… 8
人非信不立。 20
人非堯舜，… 98
人便如此如此，… 177
人無遠慮，… 187
人當使器之有餘於受，… 212
人雖賢，… 101
十年磨一劍，… 144
十步之間，… 88

3 畫 strokes

三人行，… 164
下士者得賢，… 16
丈夫為志，… 146
上士忘名，… 76
上善若水。 6
凡有角者無上齒，… 100

凡作人貴直，… 214

凡事之不近人情者，… 79

凡學之道，… 165

千古興亡多少事，… 123

千里始足下，… 190

大人不華，… 21

大人者，… 5

大江東去，… 121

大匠無棄材，… 96

大勇若怯，… 59

大寒既至，… 72

大道不稱，… 188

大道之行也，… 120

大道如青天，… 114

子在川上曰： 170

小人溺於水，… 40

小不忍則亂大謀。 185

小時了了，… 79

山不讓塵，… 190

山中何所有？ 62

山抱玉，… 60

己先則援之，… 65

己所不欲，… 65

弓調而後求勁焉，… 92

才苟適治，… 103

4 畫 strokes

不入虎穴，… 193

不失其所者久，… 2

不立異以為高，… 48

不吐剛以茹柔，… 34

不知無害於君子，… 101

不知溪水長，… 192

不恬不愉，… 56

不能則學，… 158

不患人之不己知，… 70

不惜歌者苦，… 137

不著一字，… 218

不精不誠，… 215

不榮通，… 47

不遷怒，… 31

不興其藝，… 159

不隨俗而雷同，… 52

仁者以其所愛及其所不愛。 64

仁者必有勇，… 82

今人不見古時月，… 121

內不可以阿子弟，… 83

公道世間唯白髮，… 119

升峻者患於垂上而力不足。 195

反身而誠，… 22

天下有大勇者，… 35

天下皆知取之為取，… 67
天下理無常是，… 154
天之道，… 118
天生我材必有用，… 145
天地無全功，… 102
天將降大任於斯人也，… 112
少小離家老大回，… 151
少日功名空自許， 142
少年安得長少年，… 171
少則志一而難忘，… 168
尺有所短，… 179
心之孔嘉，… 213
心有千載憂，… 114
文以行立，… 213
文章易作，… 217
文變染乎世情，… 216
日出而作，… 62
日有短長，… 174
毛羽未成，… 182
水至清則無魚，… 136
水則載舟，… 206
水流下，… 61
以人言善我，… 51
以五十步笑百步。 155
以天下與人易，… 87

以玉為石者，… 68
以財交者，… 136
以得為在民，… 26
以義死難，… 11
以德防患，… 3
以簡制煩惑，… 198
以權利合者，… 133

5 畫 strokes

世有毋望之福，… 177
世有伯樂，… 69
出其言善，… 39
功成不受爵，… 63
功名畫地餅，… 47
功無大乎進賢。 85
去者日以疏，… 170
可以速而速，… 53
可與言而不與之言，… 38
可憐無定河邊骨，… 146
古之至人，… 25
古之君子，… 27
古之所謂得志者，… 49
古之學者為己，… 159
古來存老馬，… 109
古者言之不出，… 20

四海之內，…	135
失火之家，…	196
巧詐不如拙誠。	74
布穀鳴於孟夏，…	127
平生不解藏人善，…	29
幼而學者，…	162
必恃自直之箭，…	111
民之所欲，…	203
民可百年無貨，…	204
甘井近竭，…	60
生也有涯，…	169
生亦我所欲也，…	9
生而辱，…	9
生無一日之歡，…	204
用其道，…	88
用貧求富，…	118
白玉不雕，…	21
白圭之玷，…	39
白璧不可為，…	60
石可破也，…	11
石赤不奪，…	12

6 畫 strokes

休言女子非英物，…	143
仲尼見人一善，…	102
任人之長不強其短，…	101
仰之彌高，…	110
先天下之憂而憂，…	204
再實之木，…	178
同乎己者未必可用，…	125
同聲相應，…	139
名實相持而成，…	181
因字而生句，…	214
因其性則天下聽從，…	208
在貴多忘賤，…	120
好事盡從難處得，…	183
好讀書，…	160
字人無異術，…	203
安得壯士挽天河，…	203
成大事者不惜小費。	185
有一片凍不死衣，…	48
有大略者不可責以捷巧，…	93
有事不避難，…	11
有佳意必有佳語。	214
有書堆數仞，…	162
有教無類。	167
有葡萄美酒，…	142
有德不可敵。	7
有餘則不泰，…	17
朽木不可以為柱。	92

朱門酒肉臭，…	118
百川到東海，…	157
百柱載梁，…	97
百聞不如一見。	184
百藥並生，…	94
老吾老，…	64
老驥伏櫪，…	144
自伐者無功，…	17
自信者不可以誹譽遷也，…	24
至信之人可以感物也。	19
至則不論，…	188
至樂無樂，…	46
色，…	108
行必先人，…	38
行曲，…	35
行百里者半於九十，…	195

7 畫 strokes

位卑未敢忘憂國，…	141
吾日三省吾身。	30
君子力如牛，…	40
君子上交不諂，…	13
君子不以其所能者病人，…	25
君子不失足於人，…	41
君子不宛言而取富，…	12
君子不惜身以殉天下，…	28
君子不責備於一人。	100
君子不盡人之歡，…	137
君子不憂不懼。	29
君子之于子也，…	166
君子之於天下也，…	134
君子之過，…	32
君子以多識前言往行，…	3
君子以言有物而行有恆。	20
君子以致命遂志。	145
君子正身以俟，…	167
君子安其身而後動，…	44
君子成人之美，…	66
君子有終身之憂，…	44
君子有終身之樂，…	28
君子有過則謝以質，…	76
君子有遠慮，…	77
君子死義，…	10
君子見善則遷，…	32
君子取人貴恕，…	158
君子和而不同，…	82
君子周而不比，…	81
君子所求者，…	4
君子計成而後行。	197
君子貞而不諒。	14

君子重正言之惠，…	131
君子疾沒世而名不稱焉。	4
君子陷人於危，…	10
君子恥不修，…	25
君子恥其言而過其行。	21
君子強梁以德，…	75
君子欲訥於言而敏於行。	37
君子尊賢而容眾，…	90
君子遊道，…	81
君子過人以為友，…	66
君子禍至不懼，…	47
君子憂道不憂貧。	145
君子樂得其道，…	83
君子贈人以言，…	136
君子贈人以軒，…	131
君子辭貴不辭賤，…	50
君自故鄉來，…	147
弟子不必不如師，…	105
志士仁人，…	8
志不求易，…	33
志合者不以山海為遠，…	138
志道者少友，…	138
志遠學不建，…	106
我必先之，…	59
我有旨酒，…	139

狂夫之言，…	126
良弓難張，…	86
良玉不雕，…	130
見一葉落而知歲之將暮。	200
見其生，…	1
見象牙乃知其大於牛，…	200
見義不為，…	9
言不取苟合，…	13
言之者無罪，…	124
言必信，…	19
言有盡而意無窮者，…	218
言而當，…	40
近者說，…	202
近鄉情更怯，…	152

8畫 strokes

事之難易，…	154
事以密成，…	197
事有得而失，…	177
事有緣微而成著，…	191
事者，…	183
使人無渡河可，…	178
兩喜必多溢美之言，…	129
其寢不夢，…	57
呼我牛也而謂之牛，…	56

官非其任不處也，… 212

官無常貴，… 105

官達者才未必當其位，… 108

居不隱者，… 112

居之無倦，… 210

居官者當事不避難。 211

居視其所親，… 75

往者雖舊，… 189

附耳之語，… 39

抱真才者，… 45

明於天人之分，… 176

明者舉大略細，… 100

明鏡者，… 209

東村裏鷄生鳳，… 128

林莽之材，… 95

林暗草驚風，… 36

枉尺而直尋，… 186

松下問童子，… 62

注焉而不滿，… 110

物有不可忘，… 63

物有必至，… 176

物有所宜，… 95

狀難寫之景如在目前，… 214

狗不以善吠為良，… 107

狐欲渡河，… 196

狐裘雖敝，… 93

知人者智，… 71

知人則哲，… 69

知人無務，… 156

知不務多，… 43

知之為知之，… 22

知足不辱，… 23

知足者，… 23

知足者富，… 22

知者不惑，… 7

知者莫大於知賢，… 85

知者樂水，… 72

知淵中之魚者不祥。 58

金雕克木，… 97

青春須早為，… 168

非我而當者，… 133

非其罪，… 28

非知之艱，… 183

非禮勿視，… 43

9 畫 strokes

俗人昭昭，… 61

前事之不忘，… 209

勇者不避難，… 153

勁松彰於歲寒，… 73

南金不為處幽而自輕，… 14

南朝四百八十寺，… 122

宣父猶能畏後生，… 106

屋漏更遭連夜雨。 116

後來者居上。 106

恃人不如自恃也； 51

政有毫髮之善，… 207

既不能令，… 116

既有其類，… 104

春風又綠江南岸，… 149

春蘭秋菊，… 111

春蠶到死絲方盡，… 210

是非之處，… 104

是是非非謂之知，… 70

珍其貨而後市，… 180

相馬以輿，… 77

相馬失之瘦，… 105

秋早寒則冬必暖矣，… 175

秋蛇向穴，… 53

美人姿態在嫩，… 217

美玉生磐石，… 103

美成在久，… 42

英雄不失路，… 113

苟有仁人，… 91

苟利國家生死以，… 140

要辭達而理舉，… 217

計勝怒則強，… 197

面譽者不忠，… 74

枳句來巢，… 180

修辭立其誠。 216

為者常成，… 192

為富不仁矣，… 48

為善不同，… 207

為善與眾行之，… 94

10 畫 strokes

流水不腐，… 173

家貧則思良妻，… 90

庭樹不知人去盡，… 122

徒善不足以為政，… 208

恩厚無不使。 109

悟已往之不諫，… 31

挽弓當挽強，… 199

時止則止，… 153

時來則來，… 53

書生老去雄圖在，… 142

書當快意讀易盡，… 115

桃李不言，… 7

泰山不要欺毫末，… 54

海內存知己，… 134

疾風知勁草之心，… 72

能言莫不褒堯，… 98

能尊生者雖貴富不以養傷身，… 172

迷而知反，… 31

馬上相逢無紙筆，… 147

馬之似鹿者千金，… 71

馬以一圍人而肥，… 88

高山為淵，… 123

高以下基，… 190

務審其所由。 43

鳥飛反故鄉兮，… 150

鳥獸不厭高，… 61

崇人之德，… 128

得人者興，… 205

得十良馬，… 89

得其言，… 129

得時則昌，… 153

從來天下士，… 105

從命利君為之順，… 78

情以物興，… 215

情勝欲者昌，… 24

敗莫大於不自知。 155

欲人之愛己也，… 64

欲知人，… 155

欲窮千里目，… 33

淤泥解作白蓮藕，… 104

烽火連三月，… 148

猛虎在深山，… 115

盛年不重來，… 168

莫言三十是年少，… 171

莫道讒言如浪深，… 113

處小而不逼，… 54

貧疑陋巷春偏少，… 120

逐鹿者不顧兔，… 186

逢人不說人間事，… 58

釣罷歸來不繫船，… 55

魚失水則死，… 205

11 畫 strokes

動莫若敬，… 41

唯食忘憂。 173

國不務大，… 89

國以民為基，… 202

國有亡主而世無廢道。 189

國家將興，… 199

國將興，… 165

國雖大，… 206

執一而應萬，… 198

寄言此日南征雁，… 148

寂寂寥寥揚子居，… 57

眾君子中不無小人，… 76

眾惡之，… 74

異於己而不非者，… 124

晝風久，… 177

採得百花成蜜後， 117

12 畫 strokes

勞而不伐，… 18

勝人者有力，… 56

堯有欲諫之鼓，… 125

富而不吝，… 18

富而賑物，… 79

富與貴，… 12

悲莫悲兮生別離， 149

惻隱之心，… 15

景是眾人同，… 218

智而用私，… 82

智者不再計，… 196

智者舉事，… 178

曾經滄海難為水，… 182

朝華之草，… 175

朝過夕改，… 30

無功之賞，… 42

無位而不作。 23

無冥冥之志者，… 159

無憂者壽。 172

無為其所不為，… 14

然後有非常之功。 87

盜名不如盜貨。 71

善人者，… 108

善人富，… 6

善生者必善死。 57

善用人者，… 97

善始者實繁，… 194

善則稱人，… 27

善張網者引其綱。 198

善游者溺，… 43

善御者不忘其馬，… 203

逸居而無教，… 163

進賢為賢，… 84

閒居非吾志，… 141

雲厚者雨必猛，… 80

雲橫秦嶺家何在，… 149

13 畫 strokes

愚者昧於成事，… 80

愚者陳意，… 127

敬之而不喜，… 54

敬其事而後其食。 211

敬賢如大賓，… 205

極身無貳慮，… 211

落地為兄弟，… 135

落紅不是無情物，… 141

落落之玉，… 107

萬卷山積，… 160

萬卷藏書宜子弟，… 84

勤力可以不貧，… 44

愛而知其惡，… 68

愛憎好惡，… 78

慎於言者不嘩，… 37

慎終如始，… 194

溫故而知新，… 166

當仁不讓於師。 22

當為秋霜，… 51

經目之事，… 127

義動君子，… 81

聖人千慮，… 126

聖人不貴尺之璧而重寸之陰，… 169

詳交者不失人，… 134

詩畫本一律，… 218

道不同，… 138

道可道，… 188

道高益安，… 5

道遠知驥，… 73

達人無不可，… 1

過日聞而德日新。 32

聞而知之，… 110

睹木不瘁，… 201

試玉要燒三日滿，… 73

14 畫 strokes

聞毀勿戚戚，… 45

與其有譽於前，… 46

壽不利貧只利富。 119

寧與黃鵠比翼乎？ 144

榮進之心日頹，… 50

滿招損，… 15

漁不竭澤，… 185

漁者走淵，… 200

疑則勿用，… 109

盡信《書》，… 163

竭誠，… 66

蓋世必有非常之人，… 87

說大人則藐之，… 34

貌言華也，… 132

輕諾必寡信，… 38

慶雲未時興，… 114

15 畫 strokes

審毫厘之計者，… 187

寫神則生，…　　　215

彈鳥，…　　　92

德不孤，…　　　5

德如寒泉，…　　　3

樂取於人以為善，…　　　128

窮亦樂，…　　　55

窮則獨善其身，…　　　52

罷無能，…　　　208

請君試問東流水，…　　　152

誰知盤中餐，…　　　204

誰道人生無再少？　　　33

誰謂古今殊，…　　　137

論大功者不錄小過，…　　　99

賢能不待次而舉，…　　　86

養心莫善於寡欲。　　　172

嶢嶢者易缺，…　　　179

舉世而譽之而不加勸，…　　　45

遺子黃金滿籯，…　　　164

16 畫 strokes

學如牛毛，…　　　161

學而不已，…　　　157

學而時習之，…　　　161

學其上，…　　　161

學者非必為仕，…　　　163

學莫便乎近其人。　　　164

學然後知不足，…　　　166

學進於振而廢於窮。　　　156

樹欲靜而風不止。　　　176

燕雀安知鴻鵠之志哉！　　　143

獨在異鄉為異客，…　　　147

積力之所舉，…　　　96

積微，…　　　189

積德累行，…　　　191

興必慮衰，…　　　206

17 畫 strokes

聲希者，…　　　19

聲無細而不聞，…　　　197

臨河羨魚，…　　　193

雖有天下易生之物也，…　　　193

雖有至知，…　　　94

雖有智慧，…　　　154

雖有絲麻，…　　　95

鞠躬盡瘁，…　　　210

蟄伏於盛夏，…　　　58

18 畫 strokes

斷而敢行，…　　　195

簡能而任之，…　　　90

舊時王謝堂前燕，… 　　　　122

19 畫 strokes

獸窮則嚙，… 　　　　116

識遠者貴本，… 　　　　186

鏡無見疵之罪，… 　　　　132

願無伐善，… 　　　　16

鯨魚失水，… 　　　　115

20 畫 strokes

勸君更盡一杯酒，… 　　　　151

22 畫 strokes

權，… 　　　　184

聽其言必責其用，… 　　　　130

聽者事之候也，… 　　　　129

讀書破萬卷，… 　　　　157

讀書雖可喜，… 　　　　184

鑒明，…。 　　　　50

24 畫 strokes

蠶食桑而所吐者絲，… 　　　　162